"That isn't fair," she said with a faint smile.

"Neither is the fact that my daughter seems more comfortable around you than me. But I do understand how it stings."

"I'm sorry," she said. "I didn't mean to—"

"Don't be sorry." He cut off her words. "My daughter likes you a lot. She thought that Amish women would judge her for being an unwed mother. You showed her kindness and acceptance."

"Well, Abigail can see the reality of our community now," Haddie said. "She can make up her own mind."

Paul nodded. "*Yah.* And I hope she sees reason enough to stay here."

Haddie met his gaze, and her eyes softened. "*Gott* willing."

Paul saw Timothy pulling the last plank of wood from the back of his buggy.

"I'll go help him," Paul said. "I have a feeling ten-year-old boys are easier to sort out than seventeen-year-old girls."

"Thank you, Paul," she said softly.

And for that one expression of thanks, he would have built that boy a whole schoolhouse, he realized. Haddie wasn't quite so alone as she thought.

Patricia Johns is a *Publishers Weekly* bestselling author who writes from Alberta, Canada. She has her Hon. BA in English literature and currently writes for Harlequin's Love Inspired and Heartwarming lines. She also writes Amish romance for Kensington Books. You can find her at patriciajohnsromance.com.

Books by Patricia Johns

Love Inspired

Redemption's Amish Legacies

The Nanny's Amish Family
A Precious Christmas Gift
Wife on His Doorstep
Snowbound with the Amish Bachelor
Blended Amish Blessings

Montana Twins

Her Cowboy's Twin Blessings
Her Twins' Cowboy Dad
A Rancher to Remember

Harlequin Heartwarming

The Second Chance Club

Their Mountain Reunion
Mountain Mistletoe Christmas
Rocky Mountain Baby
Snowbound with Her Mountain Cowboy

Visit the Author Profile page at LoveInspired.com for more titles.

Blended Amish Blessings

Patricia Johns

LOVE INSPIRED
INSPIRATIONAL ROMANCE

LOVE INSPIRED®
INSPIRATIONAL ROMANCE

ISBN-13: 978-1-335-56743-7

Blended Amish Blessings

Copyright © 2021 by Patricia Johns

This edition published by arrangement with Harlequin Books S.A.

For questions and comments about the quality of this book, please contact us
at CustomerService@Harlequin.com.

Love Inspired
22 Adelaide St. West, 40th Floor
Toronto, Ontario M5H 4E3, Canada
www.LoveInspired.com

Printed in U.S.A.

To my husband.
You're the best choice I ever made.

I found him whom my soul loveth.
            —*Song of Solomon* 3:4

Chapter One

Haddie Petersheim poured boiling water over the utensils she'd be using later that morning to scald them. Absolute cleanliness was necessary in making fine butter that wouldn't turn, and Petersheim butter was known all over the Redemption, Pennsylvania, area as the highest quality butter available. Haddie's late husband, Job, had made sure of that.

Petersheim Creamery had been Job's pride and joy. He'd made the butter, and she'd run the front of the store. But after his death, Haddie had to take over all of it—butter making and the sales. Her son, Timothy, helped out after school, too. Haddie's friend Miriam Lapp drove Timothy into town with her own adopted boys after school each day. Between Haddie and Timothy, they kept the business afloat.

The front of the store had glass-door refrigerators for the butter available for sale, and it sold quickly to tourists and locals alike. There were loyal customers who only ever bought same-day butter, and Haddie had it fresh and ready to sell when she unlocked the doors each morning.

Petersheim Creamery was located on a side street, just off Main in downtown Redemption. A massive November snowstorm had left tall banks on either side of the road, winter having made its first serious appearance, and Haddie had been grateful for the men who had dug a path through the snowbank to allow her to get her buggy to the stables behind the shop. What would she do without good neighbors?

At this time of day, just before eight, Haddie was in the back kitchen preparing to make the day's fresh butter. It was a job that required more muscle than most people realized, but she'd grown stronger these last couple of years since Job's death, and churning the butter no longer left her breathless. This shop—every inch of it—was filled with warm and happy memories. But this morning was a difficult day—the second anniversary of Job's death. She'd hoped to not think about it, but that wasn't so easy.

Outside the back window, the sun had just

come above the horizon, and golden rays spilled over the floor, adding to the gas heat that pumped into the little kitchen. Her old basset hound, Barnabas, was lying in a pool of sunlight, his long, drooping ears reaching the floor.

The clopping of horses' hooves and the sound of Paul Ebersole's voice told Haddie that the cream had arrived from the Ebersole dairy. Paul came with his delivery every morning, five days a week. She'd known him for years. In fact, as teenagers, he'd even taken her home from singing for a couple of months—that was how far back they went. Nothing ever came of it. Haddie's father had spotted the problem right away—Haddie was outspoken and Paul wasn't the kind of man who could handle that. When Paul married another outspoken woman, it had ended in disaster, and Haddie could only breathe a sigh of relief that she'd listened to her *daet*.

Haddie covered the metal bowl of utensils with a clean white cloth and headed over to the side door. She opened it just as Paul came up the step, a metal jug of cream on one shoulder, and his opposite hand over a bulge in his coat.

Paul was a good-looking man—tall, broad, with a thick glossy beard—and since her husband's death, she hadn't been noticing such things. But Paul was reassuringly decent. His estranged wife had passed away last year, leaving him single, but Paul was set in his ways...a little like Haddie was these days. It seemed to have cemented their cordial friendship.

"Good morning," Paul said with a smile. "You're my last stop today."

The lump in Paul's coat squirmed, and he adjusted his hand to support it.

"What do you have there?"

"This—" the lump mewed "—is a kitten I found in the road all by herself and looking very forlorn."

Paul lowered the heavy container of cream to the floor, letting go of the kitten in his coat to do so. It wriggled onto the kitchen floor. She was tiny—just a bedraggled little tabby, her eyes round and scared. She looked like she'd gotten half drowned in a puddle, because her fur was matted with dirt.

"Oh, poor thing," Haddie said. "Come on in, Paul. Let's give her some cream."

Barnabas lifted his drooping gaze toward the kitten, his eyes following her with a new interest.

"You leave that kitten alone, Barnabas," she warned. "In fact—" She pushed open the swinging door that led into the store. "In there, Barnabas. Go on—shoo."

Barnabas cast her a desolate look, but did as he was told. He rose to his feet and plodded through the doorway, flopping himself down right in front of it.

"Good boy," she said, meeting the dog's offended gaze. "You're a good boy, Barnabas." She let the door swing shut.

Haddie put a little bit of cream into a saucer and placed it on the floor.

"Thanks, Haddie," Paul said as he picked up the kitten, then deposited it next to the cream. She immediately crouched down and began to lap it up.

"What will you name her?" Haddie asked.

"I think I'll name her Thimble."

"That's cute." Haddie smiled. "I suppose the Ebersole farm is about to get a new kitten."

"Unless the Petersheim Creamery wants one?" Paul asked hopefully. "She's very cute."

"No, the Petersheim Creamery does not," she chuckled. "I've got Barnabas here, and keeping a cat and dog apart in this shop is something I don't want to worry about."

"Then we'll have yet another kitten at the dairy," he said with a rueful smile. "One of the barn cats had kittens a couple of months ago. We're overrun with them."

"And yet, you rescued this one, and named her," Haddie pointed out.

"Well…how could I not?" Paul said. "Look at her."

Thimble was thin, and her ears looked almost too big for her body. Her eyes darted around the kitchen as she drank.

"I see your point," she agreed.

"How's business?" Paul asked.

"Steady," she said. "I can't complain. It keeps the bills paid and my son fed."

"And how's Timothy?" he asked. She noticed how his voice softened when asking about her son, and she appreciated that the community worried about Timothy, too. At ten, he'd moved into a rather rebellious phase that she hadn't been quite ready for.

"He's missing his father a lot lately," she admitted. "It was two years ago today that the Good Lord took him home."

"Today?" Paul's expression fell. "Oh, Haddie…"

She shook her head quickly, blinking back a mist in her eyes. "*Yah*, well…what can you do? But it's hard on Timothy all the same. Being a boy, he doesn't talk about it much, but I know."

"Haddie, it's hard on *you*," Paul said softly.

It was. She'd loved Job dearly—he'd been older, and had seen something wonderful in her when she'd thought she'd never get married.

"*Yah*, but I'm not the one acting up in school," she said, then sighed. Again, she was saying too much.

"What's happening in school?" Paul asked.

"I didn't mean to tell you that. It's private. Timothy is very sensitive about these things lately."

"I won't say anything," Paul said. "You can trust me."

And somehow, she knew she could. Paul was one of those truly decent men, but her son needed to trust her, too.

"It's only been one year since your wife passed," she said, changing the subject. "So I'm sure you understand how hard this is."

Paul was silent for a moment, and he nodded slowly.

"My wife left me eighteen years ago, though," he said. "It's not quite the same. I had more time to grieve than most people get. I'd already accepted that our marriage was over, that I'd live alone. So when she passed, I did have another kind of grieving to do—that's true—but it wasn't all at once."

"Still…" she said.

"*Yah*, still," he agreed with a sad nod. "I understand, Haddie. Losing a spouse is very hard. And for Timothy, losing his *daet*—"

"I wasn't going to say anything about the

anniversary of his death," she said. "I meant to just…remember Job quietly, I suppose."

"It's okay to talk about it," Paul said.

"And it's okay not to," she replied.

He chuckled and looked ready to reply when there was a sharp bark and a crash. She whipped around to find the door ajar just a few inches, and the kitten was gone.

"Oh, no!" Haddie breathed, and ran to the door. She pulled it open to see the kitten scampering across the floor and old Barnabas lunging after her, his long ears trailing out behind him. She could hear his nails as he scrambled across the wooden floor, and everywhere he ran, he knocked something down in his wake. For an old dog, Barnabas had a puppy's energy right now, and as he whipped past a shelf, he caught a fluttering curtain in his mouth and it came down after him, the curtain and rod together.

"Barnabas!" she shouted. "No! Bad dog!"

But Barnabas didn't seem to care, because as he rounded a corner, the curtain rod caught on a shelf, and the shelf came crashing down against another, and then another, like dominoes, and their contents spilled onto the floor. One was split down the center, and another splintered.

Haddie's heart hammered to a stop, and for a moment, she was frozen to the spot.

"Barnabas, stop!" Paul's deep voice roared through the store, and the old dog skidded to a stop. "Sit!"

Thimble was at the top of another curtain rod, and Barnabas's attention flicked back up toward her.

"No, Barnabas!" Haddie said.

"Barnabas, sit!" Paul ordered.

Barnabas sank onto his haunches, looking over at Paul adoringly. Barnabas had always been Job's dog, and maybe he just responded better to men, but she'd never gotten that kind of compliance out of the old dog. She'd had to tiptoe around the hound's feelings.

"Barnabas, come," she said firmly.

Barnabas grudgingly plodded toward her, and she grabbed him by the collar, surveying the damage. Paul went over to the window, reached up high and plucked the kitten from the curtain rod.

"Oh, what a mess..." Paul murmured, and he stroked Thimble absently as he looked around.

The word *mess* was an understatement. Besides the curtain rod torn from the wall and the broken shelves, there were food items scattered across the floor, and broken glass from some shattered jars of cherry jam she was selling—the cherry jam she'd made in her own kitchen.

And this whole store, from the shelves to the windowsills, had all been lovingly crafted by Job. Today, of all days, to see it torn apart by this big, lumbering dog was just too much.

Tears rose up inside of Haddie, and she fought them back, but she couldn't help it when they spilled down her cheeks. Paul turned toward her, and his face paled at the sight of her.

"Haddie, I'm so sorry," Paul said earnestly. "I'll help you get this place fixed up."

Haddie shook her head, wiping her eyes with her free hand. Barnabas tried to slink out of the room, back to the kitchen, but she kept a firm grip on his collar. She needed to stay in control—this was not the time to fall apart!

"How?" she asked.

"What do you mean, 'how'?" he asked. "I'll make you new shelves, that's how. And we'll have this place looking brand-new by the time I'm done with it."

But she didn't want new. She wanted everything just as it had been with Job. But that wasn't going to be possible anymore, and she knew that time had marched forward, even if she'd wanted to keep it at a standstill.

"It's not your fault," she said, wiping her face again. Her tears were about her grief, not about an accident.

"Well, one of us is to blame," Paul said, looking at the tiny kitten in his hand. "Either me or Thimble, here, and of the two of us, I'm better with a saw. I'll take the fall for it."

Haddie looked up at him, and Paul looked at her so seriously that she couldn't help but feel a little better. She pushed open the door to the kitchen and let Barnabas slink through.

"If you'd be willing to help me," she said, "I'd be grateful."

Haddie's eyes were red, and her face was blotchy. This wasn't the strong-as-steel woman they all knew so well in Redemption. She'd always seemed so capable, even as a teenager. She'd had her opinions and stuck to them. She'd never had any trouble telling someone she thought they were wrong, but these tears had just suddenly erupted out of her, and she'd gone from a calm, collected, determined business owner to a vulnerable woman in a matter of seconds.

And it was Paul's fault. He'd been the one to bring a kitten into her shop, knowing that she had a dog. He couldn't believe he'd been so stupid! But he honestly hadn't thought old Barnabas had it in him anymore to chase a cat!

"Are you sure you'll have time?" Haddie asked. "You've got a dairy to run."

Haddie always had been practical.

"My teenage nephews are visiting from Ohio," he replied, "so we've got more than enough help on the farm right now. The timing is pretty good, actually. I mean, if the timing is ever good for this kind of damage… But I have the time to put into working on your shop."

"Oh…that's good, then," she said.

"And I'm thinking I can do some built-in shelves along your walls—those will be the sturdiest option. And I'll redo the trim around your windows to match it. I'll make some deeper shelves to replace these—" he put a hand on a broken shelf "—and they'll be less easy to topple. But give me two weeks, and I can pull it all together for you. You'll see— it'll be brand-new."

Haddie averted her gaze, wiped under her eyes again.

"You don't want brand-new…" he guessed.

"Job set up the store," she said. "It was…a sweet memory."

More than a memory. Job Petersheim had been the heart of this place, and everyone who knew him, loved him. And he'd been the one

to build the shelves and arrange the shop…
it was understandable that his widow might
want to keep everything the same.

"I really am sorry," Paul said, unsure of
what else he could say.

"I know, I know—" She shook her head, and
seemed to rally herself. "I'd have to change
something eventually, wouldn't I? I'm grateful for the help, Paul. Thank you."

She was being gracious, and he was thank-
ful for that.

"Let me get started cleaning up," he said.
"You go on and start your butter. Do you have
a broom?"

"Of course," she said. "Let me get it for
you." She nodded to the kitten in his hands.
"You can bring the kitten into the kitchen. I'll
put Barnabas outside for a bit."

Paul followed her back into the kitchen. She
opened the side door and took Barnabas outside, then came back in, brushing her hands
off. She shut the door solidly behind her, and
Paul set the kitten back down in front of the
saucer of cream.

"I feel terrible for having cried like that,"
she said, some pink coming to her cheeks. "I
don't normally do that."

"No, you don't," he agreed. "But everyone
has their limit, I suppose."

"Don't worry, I won't be subjecting you to that again," she said with a reassuring smile. "I'd best get that butter started."

She was back in control. He should be glad of that.

"I'll clean up out there," he said. He'd do his best to have most of it done by the time she had to open up shop.

Paul headed back to the storefront and spent the next few minutes picking up broken glass and tossing it into a cardboard box, and then he picked up the broken shelves and carried them outside to his wagon, piling the wood beside the empty metal milk containers that were waiting to be brought back to the dairy for sterilization.

When he'd finished sweeping out the last of the shop, and cleaning up the sticky preserves from the floor, he came back into the kitchen and put the broom and bucket in the corner. Haddie stood in front of a large metal butter churn, and she was turning a handle in a slow, even motion. A sloshing sound came from inside the churn, and Haddie looked over her shoulder at him.

"It's cleaned up," Paul said. "I'm going to head on back to the farm, and I'll be back this afternoon with some wood and tools to get started on those shelves for you."

"Are you sure they won't miss you?" she asked.

"Hardly," he replied with a grin. "Like I said, we've got two extra teenage boys helping out."

He put on his coat, and then scooped up Thimble, who had curled up and fallen asleep next to the saucer on the floor, and he tucked her back inside his coat.

"I'll be back later—you can count on it!" he said.

Haddie's movements didn't alter a whit, but she gave him a nod.

"I'll see you then," she said. "Do you mind letting Barnabas back in?"

The churn continued to slosh as Paul stepped outside. Barnabas was lying inside a doghouse just by the door. He looked down at the poor dog and held the door open for him.

"Thank you, Paul. I'll see you later," she said, and Paul pulled the door shut again. Stoic, strong, determined Haddie Petersheim had burst into tears. And it wasn't that he liked to see a woman sad—quite the opposite! Those tears had spurred him into making things better for her just as quickly as he could. But he'd never seen Haddie Petersheim vulnerable before...ever.

She'd been the strong one, even when they

were teens. She'd sat him down and told him that it simply wouldn't work between them romantically, and he'd best find a different girl to court. It hadn't seemed to touch her heart in the least back then. Haddie had a peculiar kind of strength. And today, it had cracked.

The ride back to the dairy was a rattling one, as the broken shelves clacked together, and the empty milk tins did the same. Thimble curled up inside his coat and fell asleep, her stomach now full of cream. He was already attached to the little creature, and while the last thing Ebersole Dairy needed was another cat, he didn't think they had much choice. When *Gott* threw a kitten into a man's path, there was little else to be done but to pick it up and bring it home.

Paul pulled into the long drive that led up to the large, three-story farmhouse with an in-law extension that came out one side. That in-law extension was where Paul lived, and his brother, Josh, and his family occupied the big house. It provided some privacy for both of them.

Beyond the house were two large barns— the milking barn, and the hay barn. They had a herd of fifty dairy cows being milked, and seventy-five finisher cows to be sold for meat.

It was a large farm by Amish standards, and it took both brothers and Paul's nieces and nephews working together to keep the farm running. But with the two extra teenagers in the mix—Hiram and Joel—Paul was starting to appreciate the fact that he was getting older. Gone were the days when he could lift as much or work as long as a strong, eighteen-year-old young man. Hiram and Joel worked with Josh's son Abel, hauling hay, milking and mucking out stalls, so there was certainly time for Paul to help out Haddie in her time of need. *Gott* always provided.

Paul would have to explain himself to Josh, though, and he wasn't relishing that thought. His brother would likely find it hilarious that he'd singlehandedly, with the help of a tiny kitten, demolished the inside of a woman's store.

There was another buggy parked out front of the house, the horse still hitched and munching oats from a feed bag. It was a little past ten, so not late in the day, and Paul kept the horses moving past the house, meaning to head toward the dairy barn to unload the broken wood and the milk tins.

"Uncle Paul!" a deep voice called, and Paul turned to see Hiram loping in his direction. The young man waved, and Paul reined in the horses. "You've got someone waiting to see you in the house."

"Oh, *yah*?" Paul twisted, looking in that direction. "Who?"

"A lady." Hiram shrugged. "So I can take the wagon for you."

The young man's gaze turned in curiosity to the broken shelves in the back.

"Put the broken wood on the bonfire pile," Paul said. "If you don't mind."

"*Yah*, no problem," Hiram replied, and as Paul jumped down, Hiram hoisted himself up into the seat. He flicked the reins and the horses started forward again, and Paul headed toward the house. He didn't often get visitors for him exclusively, so he was curious as to who would drop by.

Paul let himself in the side door and fished Thimble out of his coat, smoothing his hand over her tiny body. Then he headed on into the big kitchen. His sister-in-law, Lorena, had a whole counter lined with muffins and cookies cooling on racks.

"Hello," he said, and he stopped short as he rounded the corner. There, sitting at one end of the kitchen table with a mug of tea in front of her, was Cecily Peachy, his mother-in-law.

They had an uneasy truce, the two of them. She'd always blamed him for Leah running away, and he'd blamed her for not being more supportive in his short, rocky marriage.

The kitten squirmed, and he looked down at her affectionately.

"I came across this little thing in the road," Paul said to Lorena.

"Another cat?" Lorena sighed, but she came forward and took her from Paul's hands. She smiled faintly, and stroked the kitten. "Let's get you in front of the stove…"

Lorena was a kind woman, and Paul had appreciated that about her over the years. She had a big heart that opened to stray cats and stray brothers-in-law alike.

"Hiram said you came by to see me?" Paul asked, turning toward Cecily.

"*Yah*, I did." Cecily rose to her feet. "This conversation might require some privacy, though." She glanced over her shoulder toward Lorena. "I don't mean to be rude, Lorena, and I thank you for the tea. It's just that this is the kind of thing that if Paul wants to share it, it needs to come from him."

Lorena raised her eyebrows and shot Paul a curious look.

"Feel free to use the sitting room," Lorena said.

This was all very ominous, and Paul nodded in the direction of the sitting room. "This way."

The broad sitting room was bright with morning sunlight, and the wooden floor must have been newly cleaned because it smelled of wood oil. Outside the main window, sun sparkled on the snow, which was crossed and recrossed with children's footprints.

He gestured to a chair for Cecily, but she didn't sit. Instead she swallowed a couple of times.

"So what's the problem?" Paul asked. "What's going on?"

"I hid something from you," she said, and Cecily shrugged weakly. "And it's time I told you about it."

"Oh?" Paul eyed her uncertainly. "What did you hide?"

"You see, you and Leah had such a tumultuous relationship," Cecily said. "And I was partly to blame. I could see that she was a girl with a very strong personality, and I should have done more to prepare her for marriage. But I thought the two of you would sort it out, with a little privacy."

"Okay…" Paul wasn't sure what to say to that.

"Anyway," Cecily went on. "Leah was very unhappy, and when she left you, she was furious with me, too, because every time she wanted to leave you before, I wouldn't allow her to come back home. I said she had to go work things out with you. I thought it was for the best."

"She tried to leave me more than once?" he asked with a frown. "When was that?"

"About four or five months after the wedding, but that's not the thing I hid..." Cecily said weakly. "I'm just explaining why. Anyway, when she did leave, she was angry with me and she cut me off completely, even though the community hadn't shunned her yet. I had no idea where she was or what she was doing, so when she did start contacting me again, and she asked me to keep her secrets—" Cecily's eyes misted.

"What secrets?" Paul pressed, and his voice stuck in his throat.

"Her daughter..." Cecily licked her lips. "Your daughter."

Paul stared at the older woman in disbelief. "What?"

"She was pregnant—barely—when she left," Cecily said softly. "She only contacted me after the baby was born, and she asked me to keep her secret. She was shunned then, so me talking to her was very much against the rules. If I had told you, Leah would have been furious. I would have gotten in trouble, too, and I still had hopes of her returning to the community. I told myself that when Leah came home, then you'd know. Besides, if you knew about your daughter out there, what would you have even done?"

"And when Leah died in that car accident, you couldn't tell me then?" he demanded.

"When she died, Leah had put in her will that your daughter should go stay with one of her good friends," Cecily said. "And I would have told you about her then, but when I tried to reach out to that woman, I was told that Abigail had run away. I left my contact information, and nothing ever came of it."

"You could have told me, anyway!" Paul said, shaking his head. "I could have done something!"

"Done what?" Cecily asked. "I tried."

"So I have a daughter out there somewhere?" he asked, shaking his head. "A… teenage daughter?"

"You do. Her name is Abigail," Cecily said quietly. "And she's not exactly 'out there somewhere.' She's at my home."

"Oh…" His heartbeat was catching up again, and he felt his head start to swim.

"I was contacted by a woman in social services, and she said my granddaughter needed help," Cecily said. "So I went with her directly into the city, and that's the first time I even saw Abigail since she was about two years old."

Paul was silent. This was a lot of information to take in, and none of it had even hit his emotions yet. Everything felt numb.

"You saw my daughter, then?" he said. "When she was little?"

"I hid it, but yes," she replied. "Leah brought her to see me and she even took a picture of us together. I was already going against a shunning, so having my picture taken only made it worse, but Leah pleaded for one—" Cecily pressed her lips together. "Then Leah and Abigail left, and I abided by the shunning ever after. It was a moment of weakness that I never spoke of."

Paul nodded. "And now?"

"The reason why Abigail needs help so desperately," Cecily went on, "is that she has a baby girl. She left her baby on the doorstep of the Hochstetler farm, and when she tried to find her child again, they wouldn't give her her baby back unless she had some support. That's where I came in. She'll stay with me, and I'll help her with the little one."

Paul's heart hammered in his throat. "I have a seventeen-year-old daughter who is a single mother to a baby girl of her own, and she's at your home."

"*Yah*, that sums it up," Cecily said with a nod.

Paul sank into the chair, this new information spinning through his head. He had a daughter? Leah had been hiding a child from him all these years? And then his gaze sharpened as he looked at Cecily.

"You hid this from me all these years?" he asked. What use was their community if they couldn't trust each other to do the right thing?

"I couldn't tell you!" Cecily said.

"I have a child!" Paul boomed. "And you didn't tell me that!"

"I had a child, too!" Cecily snapped back. "And I was doing the best I could for her!"

"Does my daughter even know I exist?" Paul asked. "What did Leah tell her about me?"

"I don't think Leah told her anything," Cecily replied. "It was me who told her who you were."

That was something… At least someone had told the girl.

"I need to take care of her…" Paul's mind was already jumping ahead to his responsibilities. "She can come here and stay with me. I have room in my living area—I can sort out a second bedroom from the sitting room. And the baby—"

"She's staying with me right now," Cecily said firmly. "That was the deal we made with social services. She'd come stay with me, and I'd help her with the baby. We can't exactly change that. There will be social-services visits to check up on everything. But you do need to come and meet her."

Paul nodded a couple of times. "Can I come now?"

"Yes, of course," Cecily said. "Abigail wants to meet you. She understands that you never knew about her existence, and she's mostly nervous that a daughter with a baby of her own won't be good news to you—"

"That's ridiculous!" he snapped. "I have a daughter…and a granddaughter," he said, his voice shaking. "This is amazing news! I have a family of my own…"

Cecily nodded. "I'm glad, and, Paul, if you could do me one favor?"

Cecily wasn't exactly deserving of favors right now.

"What's that?" he asked reluctantly.

"If we could keep our differences between us, I'd appreciate it," Cecily said. "Abigail has been through a lot, and she needs love and stability, not to be caught in the middle of any bitter feelings between you and me."

"You mean, you want me not to mention that you hid her existence from me," he said.

"That might be hard to avoid," Cecily said. "I'd like to not mention exactly how much you resent me for it."

For a moment, their gazes met, and he could see the determination in the older woman's eyes. She wouldn't back down...and she wouldn't apologize.

"Okay, fine," he agreed. "I have to explain some things to my family here, so I'll be a few minutes, and then I'll come by your place. Will that be okay?"

"It will be just fine, Paul," Cecily said, and she smiled faintly. "I'll see you then."

Cecily headed for the kitchen to exit through the side door, and Paul followed her. When he came through the kitchen, he found Lorena staring at him, her eyes wide and her mouth pressed into a thin line.

Had she overheard?

"I'll see you later, Cecily," he said.

"Yes," Cecily said. "I feel better now." Her gaze swung over to Lorena again. "Goodbye. I'll see you again soon, I'm sure."

Paul shut the door, and for a moment he stood there, frozen.

"What was that?" Lorena asked.

"I have news…"

More than news, he had a daughter. A child of his own. A family! He'd spent the last eighteen years living single, making do with nieces and nephews and being the family's morality tale about the importance of choosing the right spouse. And all this time, he'd had a daughter? He could have had more in his life than mistakes!

He wasn't sure what he felt right now. It was a mixture of hope for a relationship with her, grief over all those lost years and deep down, underneath it all, there was a simmering hurt. There were people who had hidden this from him.

I'm a daet, he said silently to himself. *And a grandfather…*

"I should get Josh in here," Paul said. "You should hear the details together."

Chapter Two

The morning slid by with Haddie's regular routine. She opened the store, served her earliest customers and chatted with a few of them. Everyone noticed the state of the store, of course, and she had to tell and retell the story until old Barnabas looked thoroughly guilty every time the bell over the door tinkled.

"You didn't mean to, Barnabas," she said to him, giving his head a pet. "It's okay, old boy."

But Barnabas still looked up at her with the saddest eyes until she gave him a biscuit just to make him feel better.

When the stream of customers slowed to a stop, Haddie went back into the kitchen to get to work on the butter again. She washed her hands thoroughly, and then rinsed off another batch of curds from the churn, letting fresh water run through it to wash out the buttermilk. The washing stage was important—it purified the butter's taste, keeping it sweet. Haddie used wooden paddles to press the last of the water out of this batch of butter. The butter was a soft, golden yellow—not quite so dark a yellow as it was in the summer months, but still an appetizing shade. She pressed it with the paddles, gathering up the crumbs of butter and bringing them to the main lump. Normally butter was best in the spring and summer, when the cattle had fresh grass to graze on, but the milk cows at Ebersole Dairy were very well cared for, and their milk stayed sweet.

This was to be an herb butter, with fresh thyme and dill. It was her own personal favorite, and it sold very well. She continued to work the butter with the paddles until she was satisfied that the water had been squeezed out, and then she reached for sea salt and a little bowl of dried herbs.

A bell tinkled above the door out in the store, and she put down the paddles and grabbed a towel to wipe her hands.

"Coming!" she called.

Barnabas pushed himself to his feet and plodded after her out into the store, the tags on his collar jangling.

"Oh, my, Haddie!" Ellen Troyer gasped. "What happened here? Were you robbed?"

Yes, she'd heard this all morning.

"No, not robbed," Haddie said. "Barnabas, here, took it into his head to chase a kitten. So there was a lot of damage done."

"It looks that way. What will you do?" Ellen asked.

"Paul Ebersole was the one with the kitten," Haddie said. "So he's offered to help me fix it back up again."

"What happened?" Ellen asked with a sparkle in her eyes.

Haddie told the story as simply as possible—a bedraggled kitten in need of cream, and a very naughty basset hound who decided to make a point of his own.

"Oh, Paul..." Ellen said thoughtfully, and she nodded. "He's properly single now. He could use a wife."

"Then he should get married," Haddie replied with exaggerated innocence. Ellen Troyer had been trying to convince Haddie to remarry for the last several months, and she'd been suggesting any man who was single, but hadn't seemed to think of Paul until now.

"That would be a shame to let him be snapped up by another woman," Ellen replied.

"There aren't that many single men about, you know."

"It wouldn't be a shame at all," Haddie replied. "He should find a sweet young wife. Besides, I'm not interested in a husband my own age. I'm better with an older husband. I know myself."

"So you keep saying," Ellen said with a small smile. "Didn't Paul take you home from singing back in the day? He did! I remember it! Whatever happened between you?"

Her father was what had happened. He'd sat her down and explained to her that some natures didn't go well together, and Paul Ebersole was the kind of man who went along with a stronger woman but lived to resent it later. Her *daet* had seen it happen with his own brother, and again with a cousin. So Haddie had broken things off, and Paul had gone on to take Leah home from singing instead.

"He's still rather handsome," Ellen said. "He grew into those ears at long last."

"Handsome or not, he's not for me. Now, what can I get for you?" Haddie asked, laughing and shaking her head. "I'm working on some herb butter right now, but it's not quite ready."

"I'll just get some plain unsalted, please,"

Ellen replied, but her eyes still twinkled with humor.

Haddie went to the refrigerator and pulled out a roll of unsalted butter.

"One?" she asked.

"Four," Ellen replied. "I'm doing some baking over the next couple of days. We have guests coming."

"Oh, wonderful," Haddie said, and she brought four butter rolls back to the register and put them into a plastic bag. "Who's visiting?"

"My brother's family," she replied. "Just for a few days, but those *kinner* can eat!"

"They all can," Haddie agreed.

"Speaking of *kinner*," Ellen said. "How is Timothy doing? I know he's been in trouble at school. Forgive me, but the girls tell me all the little classroom dramas. Is he all right?"

Was there something her son hadn't been telling her?

"What dramas?" Haddie asked as she rang up the order.

"His desk was moved away from his friends and put over on the little ones' side of the room," Ellen replied. "Didn't he tell you?"

No, he hadn't. Not this particular punishment, at least.

"Do you really expect a ten-year-old boy to

tell his *mamm* that he's been punished?" Haddie asked. "What did he do?"

"Not paying attention. Putting dead ladybugs in someone's hair. Passing notes—you name it," Ellen replied. "It sounds like he needs to be straightened out."

Haddie tried not to let her annoyance show. She didn't need parenting advice.

"I'm surprised the teacher didn't tell me anything," Haddie said. "If he's acting up that badly."

"My girls don't exaggerate," Ellen said primly.

But it wasn't Ellen's fault. Haddie was embarrassed, that was all.

Haddie forced a smile. "I know. I'll talk to him. I appreciate you letting me know."

"I know it's overstepping for me to say," Ellen said. "But I think he needs a man's hand right about now. He's at that age."

"Well, we don't have a man around here," Haddie said, then let out a pent-up breath. "So he'll have to make do with his mother. And trust me, I'm enough to sort him out."

"If you wanted my husband to sit Timothy down and give him a good talking-to, he'd be happy to do it," Ellen said. "We've raised boys of our own, so it's not like this is new terrain. Boys sometimes need to hear from a man that they aren't behaving properly. It just… It lands differently coming from a man."

Haddie accepted the cash that Ellen held out and then returned her change.

"I'll be fine," she said, but she couldn't help altering her tone.

"I don't mean to overstep," Ellen said apologetically. "And I'm really sorry if I just did. It's just that I know how hard it's been for you since Job passed, and it isn't weakness to ask for help when you need it. You're a good mother. No one is questioning that."

"I don't need help," Haddie said, swallowing hard. "I'll talk to my son."

Like she had, time and time again. There was always some trouble her son was getting into these days, and she could hardly keep up with it. If Job was still alive, he'd find a way to talk to him that Timothy would understand. Or perhaps discipline him in a way that would make a difference. Did Haddie want another man stepping into Job's place with her son?

Timothy didn't need another man telling him off. He'd been through a lot the last couple of years, and he was growing up. Haddie was his *mamm*—she'd given birth to him and raised him, and he was her greatest responsibility in the world. She'd sort this out.

"I do apologize if I—" Ellen began when

Haddie hadn't said anything for a couple of beats.

"It's fine, Ellen," Haddie said, suddenly feeling very tired. "You have a good day. And thank you for letting me know what's been going on."

"Okay. Well, I'll see you later," Ellen said, looking back at Haddie uncomfortably.

"See you." Haddie forced a smile for Ellen's benefit.

Ellen headed out the door, the bell above chiming, and Haddie turned back to the kitchen. Barnabas followed loyally at her heels. She cleaned her hands again and then picked up the wooden paddles. She looked at Barnabas, who'd lain down next to the counter.

"Can you believe that, Barnabas?" she asked. "Timothy is getting in trouble again."

Haddie had always managed to take care of things. That was one of the problems she'd faced in trying to get married. She'd seriously dated one young man after she'd broken things off with Paul. His name was Enoch, and he'd told her quite seriously that she'd made him feel like less of a man.

"How?" she'd asked, wounded at the accusation.

"You don't need me," Enoch had said. "You

don't need my advice, or my help. You don't need anything from me!"

"How about your company?" she'd asked, heartbroken. "Do I have to be helpless in order to care about you? Don't men want wives who can take care of a home and a family?"

"Hadassah, you're just so…strong."

And he'd said it like that was a bad thing. But it was just a part of who Haddie was. She was cautious when she made decisions. She thought things through. She knew what her priorities were, and she didn't need a man to sort things out for her. She'd been filled with shame, and when she'd told her father what had happened, he'd just said, "Haddie, there are more men like him out there. Choose wisely."

And there were—Paul had been another man who'd married a headstrong woman and then lived in misery because of it. And the last thing Haddie wanted to be was a man's cross to bear.

Haddie patted the butter flat and then sprinkled sea salt and dried herbs on top. She used the paddles to fold it over and began to blend the butter to get the salt and herbs spread all the way through. It was a slow process, but it was also soothing. As she worked, mixing the butter to the right smooth consistency, she felt her nerves start to relax.

She was feeling more like herself again, and just a little more embarrassed for her emotional outburst this morning.

And she'd deal with Timothy today after school.

"I suppose we're all entitled to one emotional outburst a year," Haddie said, looking down at old Barnabas. He lifted his gaze to meet hers, and she smiled. "Including you. But no more chasing kittens, old man."

She tasted a little piece of butter. It was perfect.

The bell jingled from the store again, and she picked up the towel and wiped her hands. Haddie Petersheim didn't wish she was anything other than the woman she was. She'd take care of her shop, her son and her own affairs.

"On my way!" she called.

Paul reined in his horses in front of Cecily Peachy's little house. His mind had been whirling ever since Cecily had left their farm that morning. He'd been praying about how to talk to his daughter, too, but while connecting with his Maker was a comfort, there wasn't any guidance that he could discern.

He now knew about his daughter…and it was high time he met her.

All the same, he'd been wondering how he'd approach this. Would his daughter look like him, or like Leah? Would she know anything about him? Would she be angry about his absence?

He'd tried to put himself into Abigail's shoes, but it was difficult. How would he feel if he'd never had a father, and one day after he was nearly grown, he discovered his *daet*? Would he be happy to find him, or furious?

And then there was the question of what Leah had told her about him… That thought had twisted his stomach into knots.

Paul unhitched the horses as quickly as he could and sent them into the corral next to Cecily's stable. There was some hay in there, and a water trough, and he exhaled a sigh that hung in the cold air.

In a way he was glad he hadn't had any more time to worry over it. He'd meet his daughter, and then he'd know what he was facing. That was all he could do.

Paul headed up to the side door and knocked. He heard a baby's cry inside—his granddaughter, no doubt—and then the door opened to reveal Cecily in a gray work apron, dusted with flour.

"Welcome," Cecily said.

"Thank you." Paul stomped the snow off his boots and came inside. He hung up his coat and stepped out of his boots, then rubbed his palms down the front of his pants.

"I hope you'll keep in mind all she's been through," Cecily said quietly. "If we'd like to keep her here where it's safe and she has support—if we don't want her running away again, which she seems very good at doing—then we can't put any stress on her."

"I'm not going to add any stress," he said quietly. "This is my daughter, Cecily. I want what's best for her, too."

Cecily met his gaze, and he saw the flicker of a fight in her glittering eyes. But if she wanted to call all the shots when it came to Abigail, she'd best rethink that. He had a right to know his daughter. Maybe the next time Abgail ran, she'd come to her own *daet*. Was Cecily considering that?

A young woman in blue jeans and a pink knit sweater came down the stairs with a baby in her arms. Abigail wasn't overly tall, and she looked slim—too slim. She should eat more, he decided. And she did look like Leah…so much like Leah. A lump rose in his throat, and he swallowed hard.

Cecily nodded toward Paul. "Abigail, this is your father, Paul Ebersole."

"Hello," Abigail said, and she adjusted the baby in her arms.

"Hello," Paul said, and he cleared his throat. "It's—it's very nice to meet you."

"Likewise." She stopped at the bottom of the stairs and eyed him for a moment. Those blue eyes—so much like her mother's—regarded him warily. How much would it take to earn his own daughter's trust?

"Why don't you go sit down, Abigail?" Cecily said. "You two have a lot to talk about."

"I guess we do," Abigail replied. There wasn't much warmth in her tone. She came closer and sat down in a kitchen chair that was as far from him as she could get.

Paul pulled out the chair closest to him and sat down, letting her keep her space.

"What is your baby's name?" he asked.

"Her name is Taylor."

"She's very cute," he said.

"Thanks."

Paul licked his lips. "I didn't know about you. I should start out with that. Your mother and I—" He cleared his throat. "Well, she didn't want contact with me, and no one told me that you even existed."

"How do you feel finding out about me and Taylor?" Abigail asked.

Paul looked over at Cecily, who watched him with a tense expression on her face.

"Surprised," he said. There was more to it, but Cecily was right that his daughter didn't need to be a part of that. "Incredibly surprised. And blessed. I'm very happy to know about you, I promise you that."

"Why did you break up?" Abigail asked.

"We didn't know each other very well," he said. "And we were very different. She was high-spirited and felt things very deeply. I was quieter, but pretty stubborn, too. We both thought our own way was the best way, and... I suppose we weren't terribly mature."

"So you broke up," Abigail said. "Did you kick her out?"

"What?" Paul shook his head. "No! I didn't even know she was leaving me! I found a letter on our bed saying goodbye and not to look for her."

"A letter?" Abigail frowned. "Seriously?"

"*Yah.* That's all. If she'd talked to me, or let me know what I could do to fix things..."

Would they have been able to salvage their marriage? Maybe, with the help of extended family and their community.

"I did the same thing to Taylor's dad," Abigail said, her voice low. "I didn't know that Mom did it, too. And he never came looking for me, either."

"Oh, I looked for your mother," he said quickly. "I immediately went to her family and we all started searching. Of course, I looked for her! But I couldn't find her."

Abigail looked at Cecily. "Why didn't you tell him?"

"Your mother asked me not to," Cecily replied. "She wanted her privacy, and she thought it would only hurt your father more to know about you and never see you. Besides, I was still hoping that your mother would come home again and raise you Amish, so I didn't want to upset her and push her away."

Abigail pressed her lips together. She'd have her own opinions about this.

"Let's not get into all that," Paul said quickly. "I'd like to hear about you. I don't know much… Like, how old are you? When is your birthday? What food do you like?"

Abigail put her baby onto her shoulder and patted her back.

"I'm seventeen," she said. "My birthday is in May. And I like pizza a lot. And burgers. I like cheesecake."

"So do I," Paul said with a smile. "Cherry cheesecake is my favorite."

"Mine, too." A smile tickled the girl's lips. Was that the start of a connection?

The baby began to fuss and Abigail stood up so she could rock the infant.

"Her name is Taylor?" Paul asked.

"Yeah, Taylor. I named her after a singer," Abigail said.

A singer… That was a very *English* thing to do. It was also a little bit childish. Abigail might look like a grown woman at this age, but she wasn't grown yet.

"Do you think I could hold her?" Paul asked.

Abigail hesitated, and then sighed. "Sure. I guess."

She carried the baby over to him, and he reached out to take her. Taylor started to cry, and for a moment, Paul tried to settle her, but it didn't seem to work. This was his granddaughter… He was going to be her *dawdie*. And looking down at the frustrated little face, he felt a wave of protective love.

"I'll take her back now," Abigail said, and she scooped Taylor out of his arms. She looked over at Cecily. "I need a bottle. Do you think you could get one for me?"

"I'm on it," Cecily said with a smile. She already had a bottle on the counter, and she reached for a can of formula.

"Sorry, she's kind of fussy today," Abigail said. "She's like this a lot. She just fusses and cries, and…"

"Can I try again?" Paul asked. "I could stand up and pace around. My brother has *kinner*, and he used to do that."

"Okay." Abigail passed the baby into his arms again, and this time Paul paced the length of the kitchen the way Josh used to do when his *kinner* had been infants. Paul patted her diaper gently and kept a hand over her back. Taylor settled, and as long as he was pacing, she stayed quiet.

"There…" Paul smiled.

"I get really tired," Abigail said softly. "I feel guilty that I can't settle her down like that."

"You know, in this Amish life, we believe that it's okay to need help," Paul said. "We believe that *Gott* wants us to need each other. It's the way things are supposed to be."

"I'm her mother," Abigail said. "I'm supposed to be able to do this. My mom raised me alone without any help."

Paul felt the stab of those words. Leah didn't have to do that. She didn't have to leave, to run away as if he was some brute. He'd never been abusive, or cruel. He wasn't a man to be afraid of.

"Every mother gets tired," Cecily said, and she brought the bottle over to Abigail. "And you are doing a very good job, my dear girl. I'm proud of you."

Paul brought the baby back to Abigail's arms, and his daughter gathered her into her embrace. Taylor settled in with the bottle, sucking at it hungrily.

Abigail's hand was splayed over the baby's back, and it was then that Paul noticed something. Abigail's pinky finger was slightly crooked, bent in toward her ring finger. It was slight, but noticeable.

"Your finger," he said.

"Oh, that," Abigail said. "It's not hurt. I was born that way."

"Yah—" He held up his hand, showing her his own crooked pinky finger. "I was born that way, too."

"What?" Abigail looked up in surprise. "It's a family thing?"

"Yah, it's a trait that runs in our family," he said. "My siblings all have it. Your cousins have it."

"Huh." Abigail looked up at him, her eyebrows knitting together. "That's weird."

You're definitely mine. That was what he wanted to say, but he wouldn't push things.

Cecily had been right—what she needed was some rest, some quiet, some support.

"Could I ask you something?" Paul asked hesitantly.

"Sure." She pulled the finished bottle from Taylor's mouth, then reached for a cloth and tipped the baby onto her shoulder.

"Did your mother say anything…about me?" he asked. "Not as your father, but just… about me?"

About the husband she'd abandoned?

"Yeah, she told me a little bit," Abigail replied.

Did he want to hear this? Did he want to know why she had run away and hid from him? "What did she say?"

"She said—" Abigail licked her lips. "She said you were awful."

It felt like a kick in the gut, and he had trouble sucking in a breath. Leah had told their daughter that he was awful—that must have been how she honestly felt about him. He'd wondered how Leah could just walk away like she had, and he'd gone over countless scenarios in his head over the years. Did she have another man in her life, and she didn't want him to know she was married? Did she have a good reason to hide from him?

But, no, she'd just thought he was so awful that she wanted to keep clear of him…

"For what it's worth," Abigail added, "you seem nice."

"Yah…" He let out a shaky breath. "I like to think so."

He looked up at Cecily, and he saw sympathy etched into the lines of her face. He didn't want Cecily's pity, though. She'd been a part of this.

"Taylor normally goes down for a nap about now," Abigail said.

"And you should lie down and get some rest, too," Cecily said gently. "A mother needs her rest, as well as her baby. I'll take care of things down here, and when you wake up, I'll have some food ready for you."

"Thank you, *Mammi*," Abigail said. "That would be really nice."

"I told you I'd take care of you, didn't I?" Cecily said. "Now, you go rest with your baby."

Such loving care for a mother and her baby—and he was grateful that Cecily was doing this. It was more than he'd be able to do for her right now. All the same, what about the father? Was there even a thought for him? Had there ever even been a thought for Paul?

"I'd best get going," Paul said. "I'm glad I got to meet you, Abigail."

"Yeah, it was… It was nice to meet you, too," she said. Was that hesitation in her voice? "I'm going to take the baby upstairs, so…"

She didn't finish the thought, but Paul nodded.

"Of course," he said.

Abigail headed for the stairs, and Paul's heart squeezed. He'd met her—he'd held his granddaughter, too. And yet somehow his heart still felt achingly hollow.

"Thank you for taking care of her, Cecily," he said.

Cecily gave him a nod.

If Abigail had had a father to turn to, a father to love her and teach her about her own value, maybe her life could have turned out a little differently than it had. But they'd never given him a chance.

Chapter Three

Haddie pressed the thick, yellow butter into a wooden mold. She smoothed it onto both sides of the mold, added a little extra between them, and then pressed them firmly together. The extra butter squeezed out the side, and then she expertly pulled the mold apart, leaving a perfectly formed chicken made of butter.

There were several local bed-and-breakfast locations that ordered her molded butter for their tables. It was a little something special for their guests, and Haddie did enjoy making them.

She had other molds, too—one in the shape of a lamb, as well as a hay bale and a blooming rose. The rose was the most difficult to use, since the petals didn't always come out of the mold the way they should. She needed a new mold—one with a little less detail that the butter would come out of more cleanly.

She packed more butter into the two sides of the chicken mold again, working quickly. She had forty-eight of these to make and then refrigerate. She pulled the mold apart and set an identically formed chicken next to the first. Then she reached for the paddle again to refill the mold.

She heard the bell tinkle above the front door, and she was about to wipe her hands when she heard Paul's voice.

"It's just me!" he called, and a moment later, his head popped through the swinging door that separated the kitchen from the shop. "I brought wood and tools. I'll just unload them and bring everything inside, if that's okay with you."

"*Yah*, that's fine," she said. "Thank you."

Paul gave her a nod and disappeared again. Barnabas got up and sauntered toward the door as if half-heartedly considering supervising it all, but he only ended up lying down next to the door.

She could hear the bell above the door and the sound of his boots, then the thump and clatter of wood. That happened several times, and then Haddie went to the swinging door and pushed it open, putting a wedge underneath it to hold it that way. Paul came in one last time carrying a tool kit in one hand and a saw in the other. He looked up and shot her a smile.

"I'm ready to get to work," he said.

"*Yah*, I see that," she said. "I'm working on some butter molds."

"*Yah, yah,*" he said. "Go on and do what you need to do. I'll be fine. I'm just measuring to start."

From the island where Haddie was working with the molds, she could see Paul as he passed in front of the door with his measuring tape in hand.

"Where is Thimble now?" Haddie asked as she pressed more butter into the mold.

"In front of the stove with Lorena," Paul replied. "When I left, she'd made Thimble a little bed there, and she put some soft cat food on a plate for her, and more milk. She's just fine. When she's strong enough, we'll put her out in the milking barn with the other cats and she can learn how to catch mice."

"Always a good thing," Haddie replied.

"But something did happen before I came here," Paul said, and he stopped in front of the open door. He had a little notepad and pencil in one hand, and he fixed her with a look.

"What's that?" she asked.

"Cecily Peachy came to the farm to talk to me," he said.

"Oh?" She pressed the two forms together and then pulled them apart, the little butter chicken coming out neatly. "I suppose you two are family, after all, aren't you?"

"More than I'd realized," he replied.

"What do you mean?"

"I have a daughter."

Haddie looked up in shock. "What?"

"I take it that's a surprise to you, too?" he asked.

"It's a surprise, all right!" she retorted. "Leah was pregnant when she left?"

"It would seem so," he said.

"And you're sure this girl is yours?" Haddie asked. "I hate to be crude, but…"

"She's definitely mine," he said. "She's seventeen. Her name is Abigail."

"A daughter!" Haddie shook her head. "You said that Cecily was the one to tell you? Why now?"

"Well, she's staying with Cecily for a while. I suppose she'd be a tough secret to keep at this point."

"Did you see her?" Haddie asked.

"Yah…"

"And?" she whispered. What had he felt?

That's what she wanted to ask, although it was a very personal question.

"She looks like Leah." His eyes filled with such a look of pain that Haddie's heart squeezed in response.

"I imagine you're in there, too," Haddie said.

"*Yah*, a bit." He cast her a half smile. "I also have a grandbaby—a little girl. Her name is Taylor."

"Oh…" Haddie nodded a couple of times, unsure of what she could say, but the words came out before she could stop them. "So that's why she's here. She's a young mother in need of help."

"*Yah*, exactly." Paul tapped the door frame, and then walked off, out of sight.

Haddie pressed another two chickens from the mold, and she could hear the metallic twang of his measuring tape snapping back. Had she offended him by being so blunt?

"Paul, this is good news, isn't it?" she called.

He appeared in the doorway again. "*Yah*, it's good news. It's the family I always wanted, and I guess *Gott* had provided, and I didn't know."

"Is she *English*, your daughter?" Haddie asked.

"Very."

Haddie nodded. It stood to reason. "I don't mean to pry into private business, but Cecily... What did she say about keeping that secret?"

"Before Leah passed away, it was that she didn't want to push her daughter away," Paul replied. "After she died, Cecily couldn't find Abigail, and... I guess she didn't want to face me."

"Are you angry?" she asked.

"No." The word was clipped.

"You sure about that?" she asked.

Paul cast her an annoyed look and headed away from the door again.

"Because that would be understandable!" she called after him. "Me? I'd be furious!"

"I don't have that luxury!" he called back, and she heard the zip of the measuring tape snapping back into its coil again.

This time, Haddie went to the door and looked out into the store. Paul was measuring one wall and jotting numbers into his little book. He looked over his shoulder at her.

"Feelings are a fact, Paul," she said.

"Feelings can get you into more trouble than you ever think possible," he replied.

Haddie watched him for a moment, wondering what he meant by that. What feelings caused trouble? Unless he was thinking about his marriage.

"Are you talking about your wife leaving you?" she asked with a frown.

"Most people would tiptoe around that," he said.

They probably would have.

"I'm not most people," she replied. "Plus, you told me about your daughter and granddaughter. Maybe I got carried away."

"I told you because the secret is out," Paul replied. "And I've had enough secrets to last a lifetime. I'm not the kind of man who hides away whole human beings out of some sort of jealousy for their affections. I also wouldn't keep a secret like that, hiding a child away from her father. What about the *daet*? We all want to keep the child and mother together— that only seems right and proper. But does a father feel any less for his *kinner*?"

No, he wasn't angry at all. Haddie smiled faintly. "I know how Job loved Timothy. And I know that *Gott* describes His love for us as the love of a father. So it must be powerful indeed."

"It is." Paul heaved a heavy sigh.

"Should you be with them right now?" Haddie asked. "Instead of here?"

"No."

"I won't mind, you know," Haddie said. "I know you said you'd help me, but—"

"Abigail is resting while the baby sleeps," Paul said curtly. "And... I'll see her another time."

"Oh. *Yah*, I remember doing that when Timothy was a baby," she said.

Paul looked over at her, and he didn't answer. This wasn't about a new mother caring for her child, and she knew it. This was about Paul reeling with this news.

"I'm sorry, for what it's worth," she added.

"You didn't do it," he replied quietly.

"All the same..."

So much must be stewing beneath the surface, but he didn't seem to want to talk about that. Paul jotted down something else in his little book, then flipped over a page and started to sketch something. After a moment, he passed the book to her.

"That's what I want to build in here," he said. "Built-in shelves around the room, an island with shelves surrounding it for the center, and you could use the top of the island for more display space."

It was a smart, updated look, but it would be different. It wouldn't be the same old shop anymore...

"Unless you wanted me to just put it back together exactly the way it was," he said quietly.

That was the option she'd been waiting for.

"Am I that obvious?" she asked.

"It's just understandable if you wanted to keep things the same," he said.

And yet, even if Paul re-created the very same shop she'd had all this time, it would still be built by Paul, and not by Job. Those nails would be driven by a different hand, and she was too practical to pretend otherwise.

"Things have already changed," she said.

Paul met her gaze. "It's up to you, Haddie."

It was up to her… This was her choice. Petersheim Creamery, which had been her and Job's labor of love together, was now hers alone. And somehow she'd known that Job's touch on the place would begin to diminish as she ran the business herself over the years, but she hadn't expected it to happen quite this quickly. All the same, looking at the sketch, she felt something she hadn't felt in two years—a little thrill of excitement about the future.

This was her shop, her business. And this was a tremendous opportunity to update her shop for the *Englisher* customers.

"I like your new idea," Haddie said.

"Are you sure?" Paul asked, and she could sense that he saw the depth of this decision.

"Yah," she said with a decisive nod. "I'm sure."

There was no turning back the clock, anyway. The damage to the shop had been done, and moving forward was the only thing that made sense.

Haddie had a feeling that Job would understand. He always had trusted her choices.

Paul took back the book and looked at his sketch. He could do this. He'd been thinking through what he was capable of putting together for Haddie all morning, and this idea had cemented in his mind. It would be professional, sturdy and truly attractive. She could display even more of her preserves, and in his mind's eye, he could see the glistening jars of fruit jam and garlicky pickles.

"All right, then," Paul said. "I'll get to work on it. I brought some wood to get started—it's a nice quality pine."

Paul ran a calloused thumb over the planks he'd brought with him to start the shelves. It was wood that he'd received from an Amish shop owner in exchange for a milk cow. He hadn't had any use for the wood immediately, but the man had needed that milk cow, so Paul had made the trade. Maybe *Gott* had been at work in the exchange, because here was the wood he needed, just at the right time.

"I do appreciate it," Haddie said. "I wish

I could pay you back somehow. I mean, you aren't just building a few simple shelves anymore, are you?"

Looking at her uncertain expression, he shrugged and shot her a smile.

"I don't need the pay," he said. "Besides, this is easier than facing my daughter right now."

He could measure and cut, hammer and sand. He had control over the outcome of this project, and he could make up for an accident. But things weren't so simple with his daughter. How did a man make up for seventeen years' absence? How did he connect with a daughter, when he'd hardly known how to make her mother happy?

"I think it would have been easier if I'd had a son," Paul added. "I don't think I connected with her very successfully today."

"It was the first meeting," she replied.

"*Yah*, but…if I'd discovered a son, I might be able to understand him better. I could work with him, and lend him a hammer, or take him out into the fields."

"You could do that with your daughter," she said.

"And her baby?" Paul shook his head. "Besides, the way she looked at me… She even admitted that her mother had little good to say about me. I have to find a way with her, but I don't know how."

"It will take time," Haddie said softly.

"I've already lost seventeen years," he replied.

He slapped the book on his palm and took a look at the numbers he'd written there. Then he put the book on a shelf that was still standing and pulled out his measuring tape again. He'd start sawing a few of these boards to size and he'd get to work. It was better than standing here worrying.

"What if I helped you?" Haddie asked. "What if I gave you some feminine advice now and again?"

"You mean with my daughter?" he asked.

"Not about building shelves," she said with a short laugh.

"She's very *English*," he said. "She's different."

"She's seventeen," Haddie replied with a shrug. "Some things are universal."

Haddie had been seventeen when he'd started taking her home from singing... Funny to be thinking about that now. This wasn't about their adolescence and whatever he'd felt for her then. Haddie seemed rather sure of herself, and in the face of his own uncertainty, it was appealing right now.

"I'd appreciate it," he said. "Do you have any advice to start with?"

"Just that you give her some time—both time to sort this out emotionally, and time with you," she replied. "I think you not being around is forgivable. You didn't even know about her. And now you do."

"Her mother hated me," Paul said.

"And her mother is gone now," Haddie said with a nod. "This girl has lost her mother, and she's lost a version of history that her mother told her was true. So that will be tough. Still, after losing a mother, to discover that she still has a living father who loves her..."

Paul held his breath. Who loved her... Yes, he did love his daughter, he realized, based on nothing but the fact that she was his.

"How do I approach her, though?" he asked. "The problem that hangs between us is that her mother resented me so deeply. I wasn't a good husband, Haddie. I think you saw that early on, but Leah and I weren't so insightful. At first, I liked that she was full of energy and ideas. But I was headstrong, and after we got married, I was determined to have things my own way. She was the same. I'm not saying that either one of us behaved terribly well in our short time together, but I'm someone Leah wanted nowhere near her."

"And you're afraid that you'll let Abigail down and she'll realize that her mother was right," Haddie concluded.

Haddie certainly was a direct woman—there was no gentle leading with her. But maybe he needed that right now—a friend who could say it like it was. This wasn't about his feelings at the moment—it was about Abigail's.

"*Yah*, I suppose," he said.

Haddie was silent for a moment. She absently bent down and patted the top of the dog's head.

"Does she need anything?" Haddie asked.

"She has Cecily," he replied.

"Maybe something for the baby?" Haddie asked. "Some clothes, perhaps? A blanket? That might get your foot in the door again."

"*Yah*, that's a good idea," he agreed.

"And you could bring Cecily something, too," Haddie added. "You have more than one woman in that house that you need to mend fences with."

Paul didn't want to hear that, mostly because she was right. If Abigail's opinion of him had been formed by her mother's hard feelings, then her grandmother's feelings about him might affect her willingness to get to know him, too. He'd been wronged, but he wasn't perfect, either.

"I'll have to think it over," he said.

Haddie nodded. "Congratulations, Paul, on your daughter and your granddaughter," Haddie said. "This is complicated and messy, but thoroughly wonderful."

He felt some of his worry lift and he smiled. "*Yah*, it is. Thank you."

"I'd best get back to work," she said. "I have a lot to get done."

"Me, too."

Haddie headed back into the kitchen, and he could just see the side of her dress from where she stood in the other room. He was still for a moment, her words running through his mind. With some honest advice from Haddie—and Haddie had always been almost brutally honest—he might have a decent chance at sorting things out with his daughter.

In fact, Paul needed to do some soul-searching of his own. His wife had thought he was awful, and that hurt. But he needed to sort out where he'd gone wrong. Was it just in marrying a woman who wasn't the right match? Or was there something about him that wasn't cut out for marriage? There were some men who just didn't make good husbands—it happened. Was he one of them?

Paul spent the next few hours measuring wood, sawing it and planing it smooth. But he felt a little better after having talked with Haddie about things. A few customers came in, and Haddie came out to serve them. Some had orders set aside for them in the big, glass-doored refrigerator, and others sampled some of Haddie's different butter flavors before making their choices.

He kept his attention on the work in front of him, but he couldn't help but notice when the Amish women gave him pointed looks. He kept forgetting that as a single man now, more would be read into everything he did.

At almost four o'clock, when Paul had turned to sanding, the front door opened again, and this time Timothy came in with his schoolbag slung over his shoulder, and his straw hat pushed back on his head. His cheeks were red from the cold outside, and he looked around the store in confusion.

"What happened?" the boy asked.

"Barnabas happened," Haddie said, appearing in the doorway. "He chased a kitten."

"Oh, Barnabas, old boy," Timothy said, bending down to pet his dog, who'd come to meet him at the door. "Did you have a hard day?"

"Oh, he hasn't suffered too much," Haddie

replied. "Say hello to Paul. He's helping us get things fixed up again."

"Hi, Paul," Timothy said.

"Hi, Timothy."

Timothy rooted around in his backpack and pulled out an envelope. "*Mamm*, you've got to sign that—it's from the teacher. She said I have to bring it back tomorrow."

Paul crossed his arms over his chest, watching as Haddie opened the envelope and read the letter. She heaved a sigh and looked down at her son for a couple of beats while the boy shuffled his boots across the floor.

"Why did you do this?" Haddie asked, tapping the letter against her apron.

"It was an accident."

"Are you sure?"

"*Yah*. It was an accident."

"I've been getting some reports about your behavior at school, Timothy," she said, warning in her tone.

"It was an accident!" Timothy retorted, and he pushed past his mother, his boots thunking against the floor as he headed into the back kitchen.

Haddie let the boy go, and she heaved a sigh. She put her hands on her hips, and her gaze seemed to fix about a foot in front of her.

"What did he do?" Paul asked.

"He broke a bench," she replied.

"Easy enough to fix," Paul said. "Or replace. I could make one—"

"He needs to make it better himself," Haddie said. "I can't have you smoothing it over for him. This is a bigger problem than a bench."

"I could show him how to fix it," Paul said. "I could include him."

Haddie's expression suddenly brightened. "Do you mean that?"

"*Yah*, sure."

"If I'm going to help you with your daughter, do you think you might be willing to help me with Timothy?" Haddie stepped closer and lowered her voice. "It's been suggested that Timothy is acting up because he needs a man to give him some guidance. He's taken his father's death very hard, so it does stand to reason. Do you think that you might—?" Haddie winced.

"Would I take him under my wing?" Paul asked, finishing the thought for her.

"Would you?" she asked hesitantly. "I hate to ask…but it's better to ask you than someone with a wife of his own. It would get awkward if I was relying too much on a married man. But I do need help with my son. He's at such a difficult age."

Paul nodded. "Sure. I'd be happy to."

Haddie pressed her hands together and she smiled. "Thank you. Truly. I think that would be just what he needs."

"It's my pleasure," Paul replied, and he realized that he truly meant it.

He might not have made much of a husband, but he could help out with a rebellious little boy. That didn't intimidate him half as much as his wary teenage daughter. And maybe it was just a chance to see the worry melt off of Haddie's face, but he was happy to help her in any way he could.

Chapter Four

Paul sat with Josh on the step, as the sound of Josh's son's—Abel's—deep laugh reverberated from the kitchen, where he and his cousins were enjoying pie after dinner. Paul wasn't ready to discuss his daughter in front of the teenagers, although she wasn't a secret. But he felt off balance, still—like maybe people should be judging him.

The evening was cold and damp. It would freeze solid overnight again, despite the bit of thawing that had happened during the day. Everything would be slick ice by morning. Paul took a sip of hot coffee, then put down the mug next to him on the step. Steam filtered up from the cup, and from inside, he heard another peal of laughter. Those three boys always made the most of the time they got together.

The Amish life was about family connections—husbands and wives, siblings, aunts and uncles. And Abigail had missed out on all of that. Leah's family, like Paul's, were Amish. How would it have been for a girl to grow up without any family at all except for her mother?

"Was I that bad of a husband?" Paul asked his brother, his voice low. "I mean, I know I was immature and probably rather selfish back then, but was I really that much worse than any other young husband?"

"You and Leah didn't bring out the best in each other," Josh replied. "I will say that. She knew how to goad you, and you reacted."

"I suppose I did the same thing back to her," he replied.

"I made mistakes when I first married Lorena, too. It took some time to learn how to keep some opinions to myself, and to focus on the positive instead of pointing out where she could improve in the housework."

Paul shot his brother a rueful smile. "Did you do that?"

Paul had been a young teen when his brother got married, and he hadn't been paying attention to those kinds of details. He'd been more worried about the calves he was raising, and going hunting with his uncles and cousins.

"Yah." Josh shrugged. "There is a lot of

learning the first year of every marriage. But Lorena had a way of making me kinder than I naturally was. And I always could make her laugh. We're better together than apart. I think that's the way *Gott* intended it. It isn't good for man to be alone."

"Would Leah and I have gotten better at marriage if she'd stuck around?" Paul asked.

Josh spread his hands and shrugged, but didn't answer.

Paul picked up his coffee mug again and took a sip of the now cooling drink. "It's not just that she left. That hurt enough. But Leah hid our daughter from me. And her mother went along with it. What do they think of me?"

"No one thinks you're some sort of monster," Josh replied.

"Cecily had seventeen years to come clean. She never did."

"I think it was a selfish move on Leah's part," Josh replied. "There is no middle ground with Amish and *English*, and putting a child in the position to choose one life over another… Maybe she was afraid that Abigail would choose an Amish life if she knew you. Maybe she didn't want to share her. Leah was shunned. There would have been some very hard feelings there."

"Abigail said that her mother described me as awful." Paul looked over at his brother.

"You aren't awful." Josh shook his head. "I don't know what else to say. You know yourself. You're hardworking, honest, *Gott*-fearing and a good friend and neighbor. If you had some glaring moral failing, I wouldn't have had you living here with my family all this time."

"So where did I go wrong?" he asked quietly.

"You married the wrong woman." Josh put a hand on Paul's shoulder in a brief squeeze before letting it drop again. "That's it. You remember how *Daet* used to tell us about how to choose a girl. It seemed so silly and narrow-minded back then, didn't it?"

"Yah..." Paul smiled bitterly. "He said to choose a girl who was sweet and quiet, and who enjoyed hanging laundry."

"Boring." Josh cast Paul a wry smile.

"So boring..." Paul chuckled. "I went against every bit of advice he ever gave and chose a girl who could go toe-to-toe with me. I thought I was so smart and that I'd prove him wrong and show him what real love was." Because the older generations couldn't possibly know what love was, could they? "At least you were smarter in your choice."

"The point is, this is why the marriage choice is so important," Josh said. "I tell my *kinner* all the time that the most important choice they'll ever make is who they marry. That is the person who will build them up, or tear them down. It's the person who they will face all the good times and bad with. And like you've experienced, if you make a poor choice, there is no undoing it."

Because marriage was for life. There was no divorce for the Amish. Paul nodded somberly, his gaze moving over the outline of the spruce trees that were planted by the road to shield the house from prying eyes. He'd helped to plant those trees as saplings when Josh's oldest children were still small, and they were now tall and bushy...and the *kinner* were now adults. Time had flown by.

"But, Paul, you should marry again."

Paul looked over at his brother to find Josh regarding him seriously.

"Do you think I'm capable of following *Daet*'s advice this time around?" Paul asked with a low laugh. "I'm not so sure."

"Why not?" Josh shrugged. "There are plenty of single women who got passed over. Find one who is quiet and kind, and marry her."

"Just like that." Paul cast his brother an annoyed look.

"It doesn't need to be complicated," Josh replied.

"I have a daughter to worry about right now," Paul reminded his brother. "And by the looks of things, her life has been a difficult one. She hardly knows me, but she does need a *daet*."

"All *kinner* need a *daet*," Josh murmured.

The door opened behind them and Lorena came out with a thick shawl wrapped around her shoulders. Lorena was pleasantly plump with an easy smile. She had Thimble in her arms, nestled inside the folds of that shawl.

"Am I interrupting?" she asked.

"Not at all," Josh said, casting his wife a smile. "Tell the boys to do the dishes tonight. With all that energy, they should put it to good use."

"I asked the boys to help Sarah and Martha clean up." Lorena sank onto the porch swing, one hand absently stroking the kitten's head. "I'm sure they'll sort it out between them."

Lorena met her husband's gaze and they both smiled.

"So, Paul, when do we get to meet your daughter?" Lorena asked. "I'm looking forward to seeing her. I can help her make some Amish dresses, and we can cook together—"

"She's not Amish." Paul gave his sister-in-law an apologetic look. "She's very, very *English*. She doesn't look like one of our girls."

He remembered her jeans and pink sweater, and her way of holding herself, as if she'd never worn a dress in her life. It struck him now that she might not have. *Englisher* girls weren't raised with the same expectations.

"With the right clothes, I'm sure she'd blend in," Lorena countered. "And I have a lot of extra fabric."

"I'm not sure she wants to blend in with us," Paul replied. "And I'm a little afraid to bring it up just yet, quite honestly. We might have to hold off on that."

"Of course," Lorena said. "I didn't mean it as pressure. I just have a new niece…and I like that."

Paul smiled. When Abigail was ready, she'd have a lot of family happy to meet her. "Things are very delicate between us right now. I was just telling Josh that she was raised without a *daet*, and she didn't seem to miss having one, either."

"She had to miss it," Lorena said with a frown. "Her friends would have had fathers.

And girls have a special place in their hearts for their fathers. It's always been that way. Think about Sarah and Martha…and Nancy. They have a very special relationship with Josh."

Nancy was already married, and she came back to visit her parents on her own from time to time, and she and Josh shared a sense of humor. Father and daughter could amuse each other for hours.

"Whatever Abigail's reasons, this will take some time," Paul said.

"She knows it wasn't your fault, though, doesn't she?" Lorena asked.

"I hope so."

But he couldn't cast off all responsibility here, either. Paul hadn't been the husband for Leah, and if she'd been happier with him, she might not have felt like there was no hope for a happy marriage. She'd given up everything when she'd left him. Absolutely everything.

If he'd known where she was, he would have tried to talk to her and apologized for his part in their failed marriage. But she was shunned, no one spoke of her, and maybe it was easier that way to make it Leah's fault—she was the one who'd left.

But Abigail's words were still rattling in

Paul's mind. *She said you were awful.* In the eyes of the community, Paul had been right and Leah had been wrong. But he couldn't let himself off the hook that easily.

Thimble mewed, and Paul looked at the kitten in Lorena's arms. She poked her little black nose and one tiny paw out into the chilly evening. Daughters weren't quite so easy to rescue as kittens were.

"Mamm?" Lorena and Josh's twelve-year-old daughter Sarah came to the door. "We wanted to make cookies. Do you mind, *Mamm*?"

"What happened to doing the dishes and cleaning up?" Lorena asked.

"Hiram, Joel and Martha are almost done the dishes," Sarah replied. "And I swept already."

Lorena rose to her feet again with Thimble still safely in her arms. "When the dishes are done, you can. But you have to use the round cookie sheet. Let me show you…"

Lorena disappeared back inside with Sarah, and Paul smiled faintly. Lorena was the heart of this home, and Josh had chosen well in the woman he married.

"A mother is important, too," he said. "And Abigail doesn't have either right now. I should be grateful she has her grandmother."

Except he hadn't fully forgiven Cecily for

her role in keeping his daughter away from him, either.

"Don't let Cecily push you around," Josh replied. "Abigail needs her father, whether she realizes it right now or not. Don't give up with her."

"You're right, of course." Paul pushed himself to his feet. "I know that. But I'm starting from scratch with a seventeen-year-old who has been taught all her life that fathers aren't necessary in a child's life. Even Taylor's father has been kicked out of her life in the exact same way that Leah left me. Abigail doesn't see the need for a *daet* for herself, or for her daughter."

Josh nodded, then heaved a sigh.

"She's so different," Paul said. "And so very *English*."

"It's not going to be easy."

"It won't be." Paul brushed off the back of his pants. He didn't want to talk about it anymore. "I think I'll turn in early tonight. I've got a lot to do tomorrow."

Josh got up, too, and they both headed back into the house, where the smell of cooking hung in the air and the sound of teenage laughter echoed from the kitchen. Abigail's life could have been so very different, if only Paul had been permitted to be involved in her upbringing. It would be so much easier for her now if she already knew him.

Gott, show me how to be the father she needs.

Haddie wrote a sign with a black, permanent marker that read, Please Excuse the Mess. We are Renovating, then she taped it to the front window. Maybe there would be fewer questions this way, because yesterday, every single customer who came into the shop, Amish and *English* alike, had asked what had happened.

The morning was icy, and when she'd sent Timothy off to school, she'd watched him slip twice on some slick, frozen-over puddles before he reached the road. Now, with the sun low and sparkling off the ice outside the window, Haddie hitched her shoulders up against the chill and headed back into the kitchen.

Barnabas was lying in front of the woodstove, and she bent down to give him a pet.

"You have to move over, Barnie," she said. "Come on. I'm putting more wood in."

The old dog stood up and moved over a couple of feet, casting her a mournful look.

"You don't suffer half so much as you think you do," she said, and she opened the stove and pushed in more wood. On the stovetop, the pot of water to sterilize her tools was already steaming.

When she closed the door, Barnabas moved back to his spot in front of the stove, and she gave him another pet.

"You're a good dog," she reassured him. "You know that? You are very good."

Barnabas had been extra mopey the night before, and she felt obliged to make him feel better. It wasn't his fault that a kitten had sparked his dog instincts into a chase. Besides, in these times of solitude in the store, she'd taken to talking to Barnabas, and they both seemed to like it. He was a good listener.

Out the back, she heard the sound of horses' hooves and the crunch of wagon wheels. She looked out the window to see Paul reining in the horses. He looked in her direction and tapped the bridge of his hat in a hello. Haddie couldn't help but smile.

"The cream is here," she said to Barnabas.

And so was Paul, for that matter, but she felt oddly shy about that fact. Paul whistled as he hopped down, and a couple of minutes later, she heard his footsteps coming to the side door. She opened it just as he stepped up with the tin container of cream over one shoulder.

"Good morning," Haddie said, and she stepped back, letting him put down the cream.

"Morning." He smiled, then angled his head in the direction of the storefront. "I can get to work now on those shelves, if I won't be in the way."

"You aren't in the way," she said.

"I'll just go unhitch, then," he said. "Then I'll be back."

He disappeared outside again, and Haddie looked out the window once more as he started to loosen straps. Then she went to the sink and washed her hands. She was looking forward to having Paul around today, and she wasn't sure if that was smart on her part. She was lonely, and she knew it.

When Paul came back inside, opening the door without a knock, Haddie was using tongs to put her tools into the boiling pot in order to sterilize them. Barnabas got up from his spot at the stove and padded over to Paul for a pet.

"So how are you this morning?" Haddie asked.

"I'm doing all right." Paul scratched behind Barnabas's ears. "I had trouble sleeping last night, though. I'm trying to think of how to connect with my daughter, but it's tough. She doesn't know me, she's a new mother and I feel like all the things that she might appreciate are in the women's domain. You know?"

Haddie nodded. "Sometimes new mothers, especially young ones, get a little tired of sitting at home and only thinking about baby care, though."

"Do they?" Paul frowned.

Haddie smiled sheepishly. "We don't admit to that. I wasn't terribly young when I had Timothy, but I used to like to take him with me and go visit a friend. Babies are surprisingly portable."

"So you think I should…?" He paused, eyeing her.

"Maybe ask her if she wants to go for a ride," she suggested. "Give her a tour of town. *Englishers* come here all the time just to see the shops and look around. I'm sure she'd enjoy it. Besides, sunlight does wonders for a young mother's mood."

"Right." He nodded a couple of times. "Her mood?"

"It's not easy having a baby," Haddie said. "It affects everything, and many women feel very low after having a baby, and then they feel terrible for feeling low, and they think something is wrong with them. So they hide it, and it only gets worse. But it's normal. And getting out and seeing other people, getting some sunlight and fresh air—that all helps."

"I think I'll try it. Thank you for the suggestion."

Haddie smiled in response and Paul disappeared into the front of the store. She busied herself with pouring the cream into the butter churn, and as she turned the handle, the cream sloshing inside, she watched as Barnabas padded into the other room, where Paul was working.

The clatter of wood and the soft whooshing sound of a saw from the front of the store mingled with the gentle slapping of the cream as the paddles in the churn turned.

"Haddie, can I ask you something?" Paul appeared in the doorway, a saw in one hand, and the hair on his strong arms covered with wood dust.

"Sure." She pulled up her gaze from his arms, hoping he hadn't noticed, and turned back to her churning.

"Does anyone pressure you to get married again?"

Haddie chuckled. "Everyone."

"*Yah*, me, too." He brushed off his arms.

"Why don't you get married again?" she asked.

He shrugged. "Why don't *you*?"

"I might," she said. "I'd have to find the right man, though, and I know exactly what I need."

"Yah?" His voice lowered and she allowed herself one glance up to find his gaze locked on her. "What do you need?"

She hoped that the warmth in her cheeks didn't show. "An older husband, like Job."

"Really?" Paul frowned and eyed her again as if he thought she was joking.

"Yes, really," she countered. "Job and I were very happy. I have a very strong personality, and I know it. I could try and pack it away inside of me, but the latch would spring open eventually. It isn't fair to pretend you are something you're not when you marry."

"I agree with that."

He would, Haddie thought. He'd experienced the worst of it.

"I think it's good to know what you need," Haddie went on. "And I need an older man who would appreciate a younger woman's energy, and who might even like it. For Job, I was always young and beautiful, and he was very indulgent because of it. I'd rather be single than be the harpy of a wife that a man merely tolerates."

"Harpy of a wife, huh?" Paul's lips turned up in an amused smile.

"I've overheard some male conversations in my day, Paul," she said. "And I think you can agree that being with someone who genuinely appreciates what you bring to the table is important. I'm not beautiful enough to make up for my brassy personality for a younger man. That's just the truth."

"Hmm." Paul eyed her for a moment. "You're certain that a younger man couldn't find you beautiful enough?"

Haddie thought for a moment. "I've been told more than once that I don't let a man... be a man. I have my own ideas. And I could try to change my ways, I suppose, but I don't think that I'd be happy that way, either. Job provided enough for me that I can keep this business going and raise my son. I'll be okay."

Paul was silent, and when she looked up, she found him watching her hand as she turned the churn, a thoughtful look on his face.

"Sorry, I got carried away there. Why are you asking? Are you getting pressure to find another wife?" she asked.

"Of course." He smiled faintly. "I'm a widower now, and everyone wants to nail me down into a marriage. There is nothing more uncomfortable to a community than a widower just waving in the wind like a forgotten towel on the line."

Haddie chuckled. "Isn't that the truth."

Haddie opened the lid of the churn and looked down at lumps of butter floating in buttermilk. She carried the churn to the sink and took out a colander. When she looked up again, Paul was out of sight and the sound of sawing had started up again.

It was nice to have him around, she had to admit. She rinsed the butter and as she formed it into cones with her paddles, she wondered if it might be time to start asking around about any older widowers who might be in want of a wife. The problem was that she was a little afraid of that prospect. She knew that finding a new marriage would involve a certain amount of pragmatism, and her heart just wasn't in it. Job wouldn't be easy to replace. He'd been a wonderful and very special man. She'd rather focus on being the best *mamm* she could to her son.

Today's specialty butter flavor included a fragrant almond extract, brown sugar, honey and just a touch of sea salt, and it was another of her customers' favorites. Her hands knew the work, and just as she finished folding the last of the honey into the blend, Paul walked past the doorway. He paused when he saw her, his gaze dropping to the butter she was pressing into molds.

"What kind is it this time?" he asked.

"Honey almond," she replied.

Paul smiled and his face colored just a little. "I don't mind saying that it's one of my favorites. My sister-in-law buys it from you."

"*Yah*, Lorena always buys a bit," she said. "Did you want to taste it?"

Paul took a moment to brush himself off, and then he came into the kitchen.

"Stop there!" Haddie said, not wanting any wood dust to fall into the butter. She took a cracker, smeared a dollop of butter onto it and held it out to him.

Paul looked down at his dirty hands helplessly.

"Open your mouth," she said. It was instinct—the sort of thing she'd do for Timothy—but suddenly the moment felt very different. Paul wasn't a little boy—far from it. And when she held up the cracker to his mouth, he took it between his teeth, and his dark gaze met hers for a breath-catching moment.

Paul chewed and swallowed, then a couple of crumbs fell from his lips. "Mmm. This is a good one."

"*Yah...*" Her voice sounded a little breathless in her own ears. "I like it, too. Timothy likes it at breakfast on his bread."

Paul licked his lips. "I've always wondered how you made it."

Did he? Did Paul Ebersole actually think about her and her butter during his days? She'd never considered that before—if her customers thought about her. If *Paul* thought about her…

"It's a whole process," Haddie said, trying to sound casual. "I could show you one of these days, if you really wanted to know."

"I might like the mystery." His lips turned up in a slow smile, and she felt her cheeks heat in response.

Was Paul flirting? She eyed him for a moment, and then dismissed the thought. No, Paul was wise enough to keep clear of a woman like her this time around. She'd only complicate his life, and he was not a man who relished any more complications.

"I have to open the store," she said.

"Don't let me keep you." Paul stepped to the side.

Haddie covered her bowl of butter with a clean cloth, and as she brushed past him on her way out to the shop, she could smell the aroma of wood dust on him, mingled with something a little muskier.

He smelled nice, and that wasn't something Haddie should be noticing right now. She had to keep her head clear—one woman had already broken that man's heart and ruined the first half of his life. She wasn't about the meddle with the rest of it.

Chapter Five

Later that afternoon, Paul stood in Cecily's kitchen with his hat held in front of him. The house was warm and smelled of yeast and baked goods. A row of muffins sat on cooling racks along one counter, and Cecily stood at another counter, kneading a large, metal bowl of bread dough. Abigail stood next to her, an Amish apron tied over her jeans and shirt. Her hair was pulled back into a ponytail, and she looked tired.

"A lot of people pay good money for a buggy ride around town," Paul said. "Tourists love it, so I thought you might like a bit of a tour. This is your town now, after all."

In fact, he'd made a good amount of money one summer driving around the tourists. They'd needed some extra income to buy a new baler at the dairy, and this had been a way to save for it. He couldn't say that it had been his favorite side job ever. Most of the tourists were pleasant, but there was something rather tiring about listening to *Englishers* chatter in the back of his buggy for hours on end. He was used to more silence in his day than that. But this particular *Englisher* girl he wanted to get to *start* talking. He'd like to hear her chatter about her life, open up a little bit.

Abigail looked at Cecily. "It might be fun."

The older woman pulled the dough from the bowl and dipped her hand into a container of flour, then sprinkled it over the counter before she dropped the dough on top of it.

"I think it would be good for you to get out a little bit." Cecily flipped the dough and folded it over, pressing the dough back into the floured surface without even looking at it.

"But Taylor is sleeping." Abigail brushed a wisp of blond hair off her forehead, glancing toward the stairs.

"Dear, you go have a nice time with your father," Cecily said. "I'll watch Taylor. She'll be just fine."

Abigail gave Paul a hesitant smile. "I guess I can go. I'll get my coat."

Paul's heart skipped a beat at that shy smile. This was his daughter—he was still adjusting to that realization. She pulled off her apron and hung it over the back of a kitchen chair, then got a pink puffy coat from a hook by the door and plunged her feet into a pair of boots.

"I haven't ridden in a buggy yet," Abigail said. "We took a taxi to get back here, and I haven't been anywhere since."

"Do you normally go out more than this?" Paul asked.

"I normally do something." Abigail shot her grandmother an apologetic smile. "Sorry, I don't mean to complain."

"It's all right, dear," Cecily said. "This is good timing. You could use a break. Go have fun."

He nodded a farewell to Cecily and he and his daughter headed out into the sunny, but cold, afternoon. Abigail looked at the buggy, and a smile broke over her face.

"This is cool," Abigail said.

"I'll teach you to drive a buggy before too long," Paul said. "We can get you a little two-wheeled runner of your own, too. But you'll have to know the rules of the road and be able to take care of your own horse."

"Will I get a horse?" She squinted at him.

"I don't see why not."

"Seriously…" She shook her head in amazement. "Do you know how many times little girls ask for ponies? And now you act like getting me a horse is no big deal."

"It's a very big deal," he replied. "But it's also part of growing up Amish."

Maybe she'd start to see some of the perks of living an Amish life.

"Can I pet the horse?" Abigail asked.

"*Yah*, sure," he replied, and he stood back and watched as Abigail approached Old Moose. She put out her hand and tentatively stroked his nose. He pushed toward her jacket, looking for a treat, and Abigail laughed as she stepped back.

"His name is Moose," he said.

"Hi, Moose." She put out her hand again, and petted his nose. "Do you ride him?"

"He's a farm horse," Paul replied. "We don't ride him—he pulls wagons and plows and buggies. But we do have a couple of horses we ride when checking on the cattle."

Abigail looked up at Moose thoughtfully. "He's very sweet, isn't he?"

Sweet wasn't quite how Paul would describe this horse. He was reliable, stable, strong and of a good disposition, but *sweet*? That was a girl's mind there.

"Come on," Paul said. "Hop up in the buggy here, and we'll get going."

Abigail had no trouble getting up into the

buggy since she was wearing jeans, and she settled into the seat next to him.

"This feels so old-fashioned," she said as Paul flicked the reins and Old Moose started forward.

"That's the way we like it," he replied. "It's nice to raise children this way. You're a *mamm* now, and you'll be thinking of those things, too."

"It would be nice to teach her to ride when she's older," Abigail said.

That wasn't quite what he'd meant, but every time she said something, he was reminded about how differently an *Englisher* girl thought.

"Horses keep families closer together," he said. "We only travel as far as a buggy can comfortably take us, unless we rent a van to take us somewhere farther. But day to day, we don't go too far. It keeps families closer."

"Hmm." She sounded noncommittal.

"It's a slower life," he added. "There's more time to think about things."

"It didn't help you and my mother," she said.

Paul chewed one side of his cheek. "No, it didn't. I'm not saying that the Amish life is perfect, mind you. It's made up of a whole community of imperfect people who are trying our best. But I think having some extra thinking time gives us a better chance at making better choices. When people rush, they go wrong."

"There are lots of good people out there," Abigail said.

"Yah..." Paul nodded. He wasn't meaning to insult the people she knew and loved. "I don't mean that there aren't very good people everywhere. But we Amish choose to do things the way we do because we think it helps our characters. There's logic behind our ways. I know your mother would have wanted you to have a very good character, even though she took you to a different life."

"My mother wanted me to go to college," Abigail said.

Paul nodded again. *"Yah..."*

He was struggling with his anger toward his late wife still. If Leah had let him be in their daughter's life, so much could have been different. The Amish ways didn't have to be so foreign for her.

"What do women do here?" Abigail asked. "They just get married, right? They don't do anything else."

"Is that what your mother told you?" he asked.

Abigail shrugged. "I guess."

"Not every woman gets married," he explained. "Most women here want to get married and have families. I think that's the same anywhere. I have a good friend whose husband passed away, and she's running a shop. A lot of women run businesses of their own."

"Yes, but, the goal is normally to get married and be a housewife, right?" Abigail pressed.

He heard a different tone in the word *housewife*, one that implied she didn't like the term, but he wasn't sure why. What had Leah taught her?

"A wife is more than you think," Paul said. "She's a gift from *Gott*. A woman is more than you think for us Amish, too, whether she's married or not. Her job is to take care of the home—the cooking, the gardening, the sewing, the planning... That is her domain. She rules it and the men take care of the outside work. A woman sets the tone for the home. And her life isn't just work. Her friendships are a very important part of making a community. How does anyone know if someone is struggling or needs help? The women find out first because they talk to each other and they build up relationships."

"What if the husband is mean to her?" Abigail asked.

Like he'd been, apparently? He wasn't going to react to that jab.

"Then the wife tells her *daet*, and he comes down and sorts him out for her." Paul shot her a smile. "You aren't alone, you know. You have a whole extended family here."

"You're talking about your family," she said.

"And your mother's family," he said. "But my family is your family, too, Abigail."

She was silent and seemed to be processing that thought.

"I work the family dairy farm with my brother. He's married to a lovely woman named Lorena, and they've got five *kinner*. Your cousin Abel is about your age. Simon is ten, so he's the baby of the family. Martha and Sarah are a little younger than you—twelve and fourteen—but you'll like them, I'm sure. Nancy, she's their oldest daughter, is already married, and she's got two little ones. You might have more in common with her, right now, since you are both *mamms*."

"They know about me?" Abigail asked.

"They do now," he replied. "They're looking forward to meeting you, when you're ready."

"Maybe a little later," Abigail said quietly.

"*Yah*, of course," he replied. "Don't worry about it. I just want you to know that you have family here. You *belong* here."

They rattled down the road, and Paul pulled a lap blanket out for his daughter to use. She settled it over her legs and looked out the buggy window.

Did she really want to attend college? That was the thought bouncing through his mind right now. The Amish didn't save for college educations—their *kinner* didn't go for that kind of schooling. They saved to buy land, and to get married. If Paul had known about his daughter, he'd have been putting aside something for her, but as it was, he wasn't prepared.

"What would you take in college?" he asked.

"What?" Abigail roused herself.

"You said your *mamm* wanted you to go to college," he said. "What would you take?"

"I don't know…" She shrugged. "Mom said she wished she could have gone to college, but she never finished high school, so she couldn't. She said it's better to have some education so you can do something that doesn't wear you down quite so much. I always thought I'd like to work in a hospital. I'd like to help people."

That was admirable, actually. It wasn't the Amish way, but it wasn't bad, either. Just so different. They drove past another farm, and then came to a stop at a large stop sign. The horse stamped his feet as a pickup truck passed in front of them, and then Paul flicked the reins and the horse started toward town at a brisk trot. Old Moose knew the way, and he knew that oats were waiting for him when he arrived.

"It won't be so easy for me to go to college now, though," Abigail added. "I've got a baby."

Was that part of what she was running away from when she left her child on an Amish doorstep a week ago? He glanced over at her, unsure of how much to say.

"Being a mother is a wonderful thing," he said. "When you are old, and your bones ache, and your eyesight is dim, you won't be thinking about a job. You'll be thinking about your daughter, and her children, and her husband, and the other people you've loved."

"Is that what it's like for you?" she asked.

Paul burst out laughing. "I'm talking about elderly people, Abigail. How old do you think I am?"

"I don't know." But she chuckled then, too.

"I might look like Methuselah to you, but I'm only forty-five," he said.

"That's old to me," she said.

And it would be. Everything would look different to her, because she was only seventeen, and young people hadn't lived long enough to get any of that wealth of perspective that a few decades could give. Young people couldn't be blamed for thinking like young people.

"But it is the same for me," he said. "I love farming. I love taking care of cattle and spending time out on the land. But when I lie in bed at night, I think a lot about the people I've loved. I think about…" He cleared his throat. "I think about your mom, for example."

"You really did love her?" Abigail stilled.

"Yah," he said quietly. "It's possible to love someone very much, and not be very good at it."

"I think I know that feeling," she said soberly. "I love Taylor more than anything, but I don't think I'm very good at…loving her."

Like father, like daughter. Perhaps there was more of him in Abigail than he'd thought. Hopefully there were some of his good character traits in there, too, though. She deserved to have inherited a few of his strengths.

"Don't give up on being a good *mamm*," he said. "I'm just learning now how to be a *daet*, so maybe we could learn together how to do this, and give each other some grace in the process."

She didn't answer him, and Paul wasn't sure if he'd said the right thing or not. Abigail was still a child herself, and she was a mother now, too. She wouldn't be able to act like a mature woman would in her mothering, because she wasn't mature.

"Abigail, do you like donuts?" he asked.

"Who doesn't?" she replied.

"Good," he said, giving her a smile. "Because I'm going to take you to a bakery in town that makes the most delicious Amish donuts you've ever tasted."

"What makes them Amish?" she asked.

"Amish hands doing the cooking, and a dash of blessing," he said with a wink. "You'll see. They're fantastic. All the *Englishers* rave about them. And then maybe we can stop by the creamery. Have you ever had freshly made butter?"

She shook her head.

"You're in for a treat, then." Paul shot her a smile.

Somehow, the thought of stopping by to see Haddie calmed his nerves a little bit, too. The Amish had community at the center of their lives for a reason—sometimes relationships needed a little extra support. He'd messed things up with Abigail's mother, but he'd do better by his daughter.

Today, he would not treat her like the girl who became an adult too soon. Today, she would be a teenage girl going to town with her *daet*. And he'd buy her donuts, and show her some shops. Maybe, in his own way, he could make up for a little bit of that lost time.

Haddie handed the paper bag to the *Englisher* woman with a smile. This customer came into Petersheim Creamery about once a month, and she bought enough butter for both herself and her sister. She always sampled some of Haddie's newer blends, and this time she'd bought two butter blends—the honey almond and the herb garlic.

"It's always nice to see you," Haddie said. "Have a good day."

"You, too. Thanks again."

Barnabas lifted his head as the woman pulled open the front door, making the bell above it tinkle. With the storefront temporarily empty of customers, Haddie headed back into the kitchen, where she'd been weighing butter. She always weighed the butter first, then rolled and packaged it. That way all the packages were the same size and the same price. The scale she used was an old-fashioned one with a spring that moved the dial on the scale. The base of the scale was a polished hardwood with a metal face—truly a beautiful piece of work. It had been in her husband's shop when she married him, and she'd never asked him where it came from. One of the things about

Amish life was that very little was wasted. That reduction of waste meant that most quality tools had a history, and she wondered about the history of this scale.

Haddie rolled the butter onto wax paper and formed it into a log. It had been a busy day so far, but try as she might to purge Paul from her thoughts by thinking about other things, she wasn't quite successful. An image kept popping back into her mind of the way his gaze had met hers when he'd taken the cracker from her fingers with his teeth.

She let out a slow breath. She couldn't go there. He was handsome, for sure and certain. And the way his gaze had met hers had sent her heartbeat skipping, but it didn't matter if he was very much a man and there seemed to be a momentary connection.

The problem was, Paul needed a different kind of woman, and she was old enough now to know that she couldn't change who she was. It was a recipe for heartbreak, and it was very likely that Paul was chronically attracted to the wrong kind of woman. Some people were like that—yearning for a type of person who would only make them miserable. There were some Amish men who looked longingly at *Englishers* as if there was any feasible future between them. It was ridiculous, and Haddie prided herself on not being that stupid.

Still, the memory of him pulling the cracker from her fingers gave her a shiver.

"Enough of that," she said aloud.

The bell jangled again, and she looked into the shop to see Paul with an *Englisher* young woman at his side. It was like Leah had stepped back into her shop—the resemblance was that startling. This was definitely Paul's daughter.

Haddie wiped her hands and emerged from the kitchen.

"Hi," Haddie said with a smile. "You must be Abigail. You look so much like your mother!"

Paul and Abigail both looked over at her, mirrored expressions of surprise on their faces. Right. People probably weren't talking about Leah around here, were they? And Haddie never had been very good at avoiding taboo topics.

"Uh…" Abigail licked her lips. "People used to tell me that."

"Well, it's the truth," Haddie replied. "I knew your mother when she was your age."

"Were you friends?" Abigail asked.

Haddie felt her cheeks start to warm. Leah had gotten Paul after they'd broken up, and

Leah had been rather exultant about her victory. "We weren't close, exactly. But we knew each other. I'm sure she was incredibly proud of you. Come on in."

"What's a creamery?" Abigail asked.

"I make butter," Haddie said with a smile. "Your father's dairy provides the cream, and every day I make a new batch of fresh butter that I sell to people around here."

"Yeah?" Abigail looked interested. "That's it? Just butter?"

"Lots of different kinds of butter," Haddie said. She glanced toward Paul, and she noticed that his face had colored just a little. Was he remembering the taste test from this morning, too?

"My dad said that he brought a kitten in here and caused all this damage," Abigail said, a smile teasing at her lips.

"He did." Haddie glanced around the shop. "But he's making me new shelves, so I've forgiven him."

Paul smiled faintly.

"Did you want to see what I'm working on now?" Haddie asked. "I'm weighing butter for sale."

"Sure," Abigail said.

All three of them went back into the kitchen, and Haddie gave a quick explanation of the stages of butter making, from churning it to salting and flavoring it, before wrapping it for sale.

"And then I weigh out exactly one quarter pound per roll of butter," Haddie concluded. "That's what I'm doing now. Did you want a taste?"

Haddie pulled out the crackers and used a knife to put a sample of butter onto one, then passed it over. Abigail took a bite and nodded.

"That's really good."

"I try," Haddie said with a smile.

"Did you want some, Dad?" Abigail asked.

"No, no," Paul said quickly. "I'm okay."

Haddie couldn't help the laughter that bubbled up inside of her. So Paul was embarrassed, too, was he? Somehow that made her feel better.

"So tell me about your baby," Haddie said. "Her name is Taylor, your *daet* said?"

"Taylor." She nodded. "She's four months old, and she's really fussy. I went to this teen-mom, support-group thing when she was born, and the other moms had newborns that just slept and cuddled, but Taylor was fussy from the start."

"Some are like that," Haddie said. "But she's growing?"

"Yeah. Like a weed. She's in six-month clothes right now."

"And what about the father?" Haddie asked.

"I don't like to talk about him," Abigail said, and Paul shuffled his feet uncomfortably.

"But he exists," Haddie pressed. "Are you still in contact with him?"

"No." The answer was curt, and when Haddie looked over at Paul, he just shrugged.

"Did he leave you?" Haddie used a paddle to scoop more butter onto the scale.

"No, I left him," Abigail said, sounding somewhat indignant. "We weren't supposed to have a baby, and he's a terrible father. He was flirting with other girls, too, and going off to parties and leaving me at home. So I left a note saying not to look for me, and… he didn't."

"He didn't even try to call?" Haddie asked.

"Nope. So that tells you what kind of guy he was." Abigail sighed. "But lots of men are like that. They don't really love you."

"But did you love him?" Haddie asked softly.

Abigail shrugged, but her chin trembled. *Yah*, Haddie had thought so. It wasn't so easy for a girl to separate her emotions from a relationship like that. She very likely thought the boy was in love with her, too, until his actions proved otherwise. Haddie leaned over and nudged Abigail's arm with the side of her own.

"I'm sorry," Haddie said softly. "You're right. Some men can be bad, but not all of them. I know that for a fact. Your *daet* is a good one."

Paul's gaze jerked up in surprise, and Haddie gave him a sympathetic smile.

"I'll be fine," Abigail said. "My mom raised me on my own. I don't need Curt."

"You will be fine," Haddie agreed. "I'm not arguing that. But I'm still sorry that he wasn't a worthier boy. If he was a good one, he'd have wanted to provide for you and marry you."

And it was a little late for Abigail to discover that he wasn't worthy of her now. That was why the Amish made sure to have no regrets when they dated. They didn't do anything during courting that couldn't be talked about openly and plainly in front of the whole community later…because gossip being what it was, it *would* be discussed by everyone later.

"My dad said that you were married before," Abigail said.

"I was," Haddie said. "My husband's name was Job. He passed away. He was a good man. He worked hard every day, and he was… He was kind to me." Haddie's mind went back to her husband's quick smile, his warm hand on her waist when he would pass her in the kitchen, the jovial sound of his voice when he told customers that his choice in wives was the best decision he'd ever made.

"He made me feel beautiful," Haddie added quietly.

Abigail met Haddie's gaze, and they exchanged a sad smile. There was a good twenty years between them in age, but there were some things women understood.

"He sounds like a good one," Abigail said. "Do you have kids?"

"I have a son." Haddie placed another roll of packaged butter aside. "Just the one."

"Taylor is my only child, too," Abigail said. "Does it get easier?"

"Not really," Haddie replied. "But you do start to realize that as hard as it is, you can do it. So you get a little more confident."

This teenager was just a child in some ways, and in others, she was very grown up. Motherhood did that. Abigail moved over to the window, and she looked out toward the stable, where Haddie's horse was contentedly chewing on some oats.

"You like horses?" Haddie asked.

Abigail nodded. "Yeah..."

"You can go out and pet them. Mine is

named Lily. She's a real sweetheart. I have some carrots in the icebox if you want to win her over with treats."

Paul wordlessly opened the icebox and pulled out a few carrots. Abigail took them with a smile and headed out the side door. Haddie watched Abigail approach the horses as she wrapped another roll of butter.

"How's it going with her?" Haddie asked.

Paul crossed his arms over his chest. "Good. I think. I'm surprised she opened up to you about Taylor's *daet*. She wouldn't say anything to me about him. I didn't even know his name."

"I took her by surprise, I suppose," Haddie said. "That, and I'm a woman. We women tend to get to the heart of the matter."

"So he broke her heart…" Paul said softly.

"*Of course*, he broke her heart!" Haddie retorted. "How could he not? Do you really think a girl that age gives herself to a boy and keeps her emotions separate? It's not possible. She might claim to feel nothing at all, but that boy fathered a child with her, and then broke her heart. No question."

Paul licked his lips. "I'd like a chance to speak with that young man."

Those were strong words coming from an Amish man. Violence was never acceptable, even in defense of a daughter. But a lengthy lecture intended to eviscerate a young man's overinflated idea of his own importance? That was not only acceptable, but it was also dished out liberally when needed.

Haddie shrugged. "I doubt it would make any difference. You're better off focusing on your daughter and granddaughter."

Paul nodded and was silent for a moment. Haddie continued wrapping butter, her fingers knowing the work. Every roll that she added to the pile made her feel like she was accomplishing something.

"I appreciate you talking to her," Paul said at last. "I could come by tomorrow to help Timothy with that bench, if you want."

"That would be very nice," she replied. "He needs to make that right. I know his heart will feel lighter once he does."

Paul put his hat back on his head and moved toward the side door. He paused with his hand on the knob.

"You said that—" Paul turned back and met her gaze "—Job made you feel beautiful."

"Oh..." Haddie went back to scooping butter, her face feeling warm. "He did. He made me feel like the prettiest woman in any room."

"He was a good man," Paul said, his voice

gruff. "But just to be honest, you tend to be the prettiest woman in any room to begin with."

Haddie looked up at him, surprised. He stood there, his dark gaze locked on her, and she felt her breath seep out of her. She had no words to answer him. She'd often thought that Paul was a handsome man, but she had no idea he'd thought similar things about her... Paul pulled the door open.

"You're just the kind of woman who doesn't notice," he added.

From the front of the store, the bell tinkled, letting her know that another customer had come in, and Paul closed the door shut behind him as he headed outside. She let out a shaky breath.

Did Paul really mean it? He wasn't the kind of man to say anything he didn't mean.

"Hello?" a voice called.

"Coming!" she called back.

There was butter to sell, but she felt her heartbeat skipping happily as she pushed open the swinging door and went back to the sales floor.

Paul thought she was pretty.

Chapter Six

Paul pulled the door shut behind him, his heart hammering in his chest.

Had he just said that…out loud?

What was it about Haddie Petersheim that made him say the things he was thinking? Maybe it was his relief that Haddie had been able to get his daughter to open up, or perhaps just the emotional upheaval of all the changes in his life lately, but he just didn't seem capable of keeping his mouth shut!

His spontaneous compliment for Haddie plagued him all that night, and by the next day, he'd made a private deal with himself that he'd be nothing but proper and Christianly from this day on.

He worked with his brother and nephews in the dairy, and when school let out, he hitched up his buggy with some wood and supplies in the back and headed toward town. He had promised to help Timothy with the bench. They'd decided to build a new one since it would be a good skill for the boy to learn.

As his buggy rattled over the bumps in the gravel, his mind kept going back to his daughter and Haddie, and how she'd talked to Abigail in a way that he couldn't. He hadn't expected getting to know his daughter to be easy, but he had hoped that some sort of unspoken bond would exist between them. He was her father, after all! But Abigail seemed more comfortable talking with Haddie after only one meeting than she did with him.

Maybe *Gott* gave girls a *mamm* and a *daet* for a reason. There were things that simply stayed in the women's domain. Not that it felt fair. He was the only living parent Abigail had left, and he wanted to do everything he could for her.

Downtown Redemption was busier than usual today. A tourist bus had just arrived, and streams of *Englishers* came down the street, pointing phones this way and that. One woman pointed a phone directly at him and tried to look casual, as if she hadn't just taken his picture.

He sighed. He was just a regular man trying to live his life, and the curiosity of outsiders over Amish ways could get tiring after a while. He knew that the tourists' interest in their way of life was important to keeping their businesses afloat, but it could be a difficult balance sometimes, especially when he was absorbed in his own problems.

Paul steered his horse into the alley behind Petersheim Creamery, grateful to be back out of sight again. He unhitched his horse and stabled it next to Haddie's quarter-horse mare. He gave them both some extra oats, and then headed toward the side door of Haddie's shop.

He knocked, and when there wasn't an answer, he opened the door and stepped inside. Barnabas was lying next to the woodstove, and he looked up lazily as Paul came in.

"Hello, old boy," Paul said.

Barnabas dropped his head back down. That old hound wasn't much of a guard dog, unless he was guarding against kittens, it would seem. Timothy's book bag was lying on a side table, and his coat was hung up on a hook. From the other room, Paul could hear Haddie's voice.

"I know it's hard, son," she said. "I miss him, too."

"Simon Ebersole says that his *daet* takes him milking every morning." Timothy's voice was full of emotion. "And Simon says his *daet* is showing him how to drive a buggy already. And his *daet*—"

"Timothy, I can show you all sorts of things," Haddie said. "If you want to milk a cow, I can bring you to the neighbors and I'm sure Abram Peachy will let you milk his as much as you like. We don't have a cow. We didn't have one when your father was alive, either. If your father were still here, he'd be showing you how to make butter. It's the family business. You learn what your parents do."

"You learn what your *daet* does," Timothy countered.

There was a beat of silence and Paul winced. Timothy was missing his father something fierce, and nothing Haddie said was going to be right.

"Well, your *daet* made butter. And I make butter. And you're learning to make butter, too." Haddie's voice was firm. The swinging door opened, and Haddie came through and startled when she saw him.

"Oh, you're here," she said with a faint smile.

"*Yah*, I knocked…" He shrugged. "I hope it's okay that I let myself in."

"It's fine." She batted a hand through the air, then called over her shoulder, "Timothy, Paul is here!"

"Is everything okay?" Paul asked.

Haddie sighed, then shook her head. "It's a tough day."

Before she could say more, Timothy came into the kitchen. His hair hung down into his eyes, and he pushed it away from his face.

"I hear we need to make a bench," Paul said.

Timothy's face reddened. *"Yah."*

"What happened?" Paul asked.

"It—" The boy dug his toe into the floor. "It just broke."

"Workmanship these days…" Paul shot Timothy a teasing smile. "It's just going downhill. You look at a bench sideways, and it breaks apart. I tell you, in my day, we knew how to make a bench."

"It wasn't quite like that," Timothy said with a laugh, then he shrugged. "I jumped on it. I was getting away from another kid."

"Why did you need to get away from him?" Paul asked.

"He was chasing me."

Paul rolled his eyes jokingly.

"With a dead mouse!" Timothy added. "He said I had to smell it."

"That's incredibly filthy," Haddie said. "You can get sick from putting dead animals near your face, or not washing your hands. Did you tell your teacher, Timothy?"

Timothy froze, looking up at his mother like a stunned sheep.

"Did you tell her?" Haddie pressed. "Because I think she needs to know the whole story, don't you?"

"No," Timothy said, his voice low. It wasn't clear what he was saying no to, but Paul recognized the hesitation.

"Which kid?" Paul asked quietly.

"It doesn't matter. It was just a game. And I jumped on the bench, and it broke. That's it."

Paul glanced up at Haddie and saw the worried look on her face.

"The end of the story leaves us with a broken bench," Paul said.

"*Yah.* I tried to fix it." Timothy's cheeks reddened again. "It didn't work."

"What did you use?" Paul asked.

"Some school glue."

Paul's heart went out to the boy. The very thought of Timothy hunched over a broken bench trying to glue it back together filled his heart with sympathy. Had the other *kinner* laughed at him? Timothy didn't know how to fix it, but he sure did want to make it right.

"Well, I've got wood, and I've got tools, and we've got a bench to make," Paul said, putting some enthusiasm into his tone. "As men, we mess up sometimes. It happens to the best of us."

"Did it happen to you?" Timothy asked.

"Often," Paul replied. "But we make it right. That's what makes a man a man—he doesn't let a debt go unpaid. And you, my young friend, owe a bench. Right?"

Timothy nodded, but his eyes had started to look hopeful. "*Yah*, I do."

"We're going to repay that debt," Paul said. "And you'll be square with your teacher again. We'll make sure of it."

Timothy smiled faintly. "Okay. *Yah*. That would be good."

He looked over at Haddie. "Do you want us to work outside? If he works in the store with me, I can keep working on the shelves while giving him some direction."

"Inside is fine," Haddie replied.

"Go on out to my buggy and start carrying the wood in, okay?" he said to the boy.

Timothy headed out the door, and Paul caught Haddie looking at him with that same worried expression on her face.

"Is he being picked on?" Haddie asked.

She seemed so worried about her son that he suddenly had the instinct to slide an arm around her. He curbed it, of course. He didn't have a right to touch her in any way, but he wasn't so different from Timothy right now—he wanted to make things better.

"He might be being picked on," Paul said. "But he won't just come out and say it, because that would be telling on the other boy. There are codes of conduct here. Boys don't rat each other out."

"Ah." Haddie sighed. "I could insist that he tell me, or talk to the teacher…"

"Oh, it doesn't need to be that dramatic," Paul said. "Just because he won't tattle doesn't mean that the information can't come out in a different way. When men work, they talk."

"That wouldn't be tattling?" she asked.

"That would be men sharing. Telling your mother is tattling." He winked.

"That isn't fair," she said with a faint smile.

"Neither is the fact that my daughter seems more comfortable around you than she is around me. But I do understand how it stings."

"I'm sorry," she said. "I didn't mean to get between you, or—"

"Don't be sorry," he said, cutting off her words. "You're a great help. My daughter likes you a lot. She thought that Amish women would judge her or look down on her for being an unwed mother. You showed her the kindness and acceptance that she didn't think she'd find."

"Her mother didn't show us in a good light, did she?" Haddie asked.

"I don't think she did."

"Well, Abigail can see the reality of our community now," Haddie said. "She can make up her own mind."

Paul nodded. "*Yah*. And I hope she sees what I do. I hope she sees reason enough to stay here."

Haddie met his gaze, and her eyes softened. "*Gott* willing."

Those words encapsulated so much of an Amish life. Their hopes, their prayers and their ambitions were all held in *Gott*'s capable hands. And *Gott*'s ways were not their ways. Paul nodded.

"Yah, *Gott* willing."

Paul looked out the window and saw Timothy pulling the last plank of wood from the back of his buggy. It clattered on top of the other two planks.

"I'll go help him," Paul said. "I have a feeling ten-year-old boys are easier to sort out than seventeen-year-old girls."

Haddie didn't answer, but she did smile.

"It will be okay," Paul said, catching her eye. "We'll start with making a bench and see how we progress."

"Thank you, Paul," she said softly.

And for that one expression of thanks, he would have built that boy a whole schoolhouse, he realized. Haddie wasn't quite so alone as she thought. He was a part of her community, and that was beginning to mean something more to him that he wasn't quite ready to look at.

Paul headed out the side door and crossed the trodden snow to where the boy was hoisting up a plank of wood.

"You carry that one," Paul said. "I'll get these two."

It would be hard for Timothy to carry the plank alone, but the effort would make it worth more in a boy's eyes. When Timothy presented this bench to his teacher, he'd know he'd made things right with his own sweat. Hard work mattered to the Amish because it was more than a way to hold families close to home—it was a way to cleanse out a heart, too.

The bell above the door tinkled, and Haddie went into the front of the shop, where Paul and Timothy were setting up to work alongside Paul's shelf-building. They could have worked outside in the snow, but since all of the material was inside the store already for Paul's work on the shelves, she'd agreed to allow them to work here. As she served her next few customers, Paul and Timothy brought the wood inside and Paul laid the boards on top of the sawhorses. He pulled out a piece of paper and a little nub of pencil, and started to draw, then tipped the paper so Timothy could see.

The *Englisher* customers tended to buy small packages of flavored butter. One bought a whole sampler that included five different flavors and a package of crackers. Amish customers bought some flavored butter, but mostly large quantities of plain butter for baking and eating. Big families went through a lot of butter.

When the customers had gone, Haddie went back into the kitchen and continued working on a new batch of orange butter—another big favorite with her *Englisher* clientele. She had a batch of churned butter in her icebox, and she pulled out some fresh oranges to zest for a new, special butter blend she'd been wanting to try.

As she worked, she listened to Paul and Timothy talking.

"So we have to measure, you see?" Paul was saying. "For a three-seat bench, you've got to leave enough room for elbows, not just posteriors."

Haddie chuckled at that, and she heard Timothy laugh, too. Then there were a couple of beats of silence.

"Do I do it?" Timothy asked hesitantly.

"*Yah*, you measure it."

"Where's the measuring tape?"

"Here—"

This would be good for Timothy, and she felt a pang of guilt that she hadn't gotten him working with another man in the family since Job's death. The time had swept by in some ways, and crept past in others. But all through the last two years, Haddie had a business to run. She didn't have time to figure out if Timothy's woodworking skills were suffering when her larger concern was keeping food on the table.

"Okay, so are you confident that you've measured correctly?" Paul's voice was brisk.

"Um…"

"Better to measure twice and be sure and certain."

"Okay…"

Haddie zested five oranges, and her fingers started to take on an orange tint, too. She added it to the ball of butter, working the zest into the butter with strong, smooth strokes of the wooden paddle. There was something soothing about the work. She enjoyed the details, too. She had a stamp with a stylized *P* standing for Petersheim that she pressed into the top of blended butter pats, and she liked knowing that the product she sold was both delicious and pretty.

The swinging door opened, and she heard the sound of the saw in the background as Paul came into the kitchen.

"How's it going?" she asked.

"He knows what he needs to do, and I'm going to let him do it on his own for a little while," Paul said.

The sawing continued, and as the door swung shut, she caught a glimpse of Timothy bent over a plank of wood, his elbow rising and falling with each saw stroke. Then the door shut, leaving her and Paul alone.

Haddie put aside the butter, washed her hands again and went over to her son's book bag, which was lying on the side table. She unzipped it and peeked inside. There were the Tupperware containers from his lunch, a math textbook and some loose-leaf pages with various amounts of work on them, and also a vague smell of bread crusts. Tucked to one side there was a white envelope like the one from a day ago, and Haddie sighed.

"Note from the teacher again?" Paul asked.

"It looks that way." Haddie tore it open and

read the contents. "She wants to meet with me tomorrow after school."

Paul didn't say anything.

"He used to be such a well-behaved boy, Paul," she said with a sigh.

"What does she want to talk about?" he asked.

"She doesn't say." But she was dreading whatever it was. Lately, if it wasn't rough-housing or disrupting the class, she was being told about Timothy using bad words, or not finishing his homework.

"I put him to work around the shop," Haddie added. "I make sure he makes his bed every morning, and that he does his chores at home properly. I don't let him off the hook! Without Job, there is so much that has to be done between us, and he works really hard. I don't understand where this bad attitude of his is coming from, because I'm not spoiling him."

"Maybe the teacher will have some insights," Paul suggested, and for some reason that irritated her.

"She doesn't know my son like I do," she said, a little more sharply than intended.

"He also doesn't act like that around you," Paul replied, sounding so calm and logical.

Haddie knew she wasn't angry at Paul, exactly, but she was frustrated nonetheless. She gathered the plastic containers from a shelf and brought them over to the island counter, where her scale was waiting.

"Well, what am I supposed to do?" she demanded, turning toward him.

"Maybe you need a break," he said.

"A break?" She almost laughed. "I don't get breaks, Paul! I'm a mother, and I'm running a shop. There are no breaks for me."

"I don't think you're doing anything wrong, is my point," Paul said. "I think that Timothy is just...a kid."

"The other kids aren't acting up like he is, though," she said.

"My oldest nephew, Abel, got it into his head that he was going to be a race-car driver when he was eleven," Paul said.

"What?" Haddie couldn't help the surprise in her voice. "Where did he get that idea from?"

"He saw some toy cars in the farm-supply store, and he saw some videos of racing cars on a TV in a store when his *daet* took him into Shipshewana for a day, and he pieced it together in his head. He was going to be a race-car driver."

"What did Josh and Lorena do?" she asked.

"Anything they could think of." Paul leaned against the counter. "They lectured and gave him reading material. They had an elder explain the importance of the *Ordnung*. They even had me talk to him more than once. Nothing made a difference. And this phase lasted a good year."

"What happened?" Haddie paused her work, a butter paddle in one hand. The Ebersoles were a good family, and they had raised good *kinner*. She'd never suspected that any of their *kinner* had been rebellious.

"He was twelve when one of the teenagers in the community jumped the fence," Paul replied. "That was when he saw the reality of leaving Amish life—the family the boy wouldn't work with, or see very often, and the heartbreak he left behind. It was only then that he recognized the price of his dream, and he came to his *daet* in tears, and he said he didn't want to race cars. He wanted to work with his *daet*. He never brought it up again."

"So I just…wait?" she asked. Just wait, and do nothing? It didn't sit well with her. Action was more to her temperament.

Paul met her gaze, and for a moment, he didn't say anything. Then he sighed. "No, that would drive you crazy."

Haddie let out a breathy laugh. "It would."

A smile tickled the corners of his lips. "But while you're trying everything you can think of, realize that *Gott* is working on his life, too. And *Gott* gets through. Always. He did with Abel."

Haddie felt some of her worry lift, and she nodded. "That's good advice, Paul."

"But that's advice coming from someone who has never raised a child of his own," Paul added.

The sound of sawing stopped then, and Paul pushed himself off the counter. His gait was relaxed, and he disappeared back into the front of the store.

"*Yah*, *yah*, very good." Haddie heard Paul praise her son. "Now we need to start working on a groove to hold these two pieces together. So let me show you…"

Haddie scooped some butter into the first container and put it onto the scale. She was careful in her weighing. She wouldn't cheat a customer out of even an ounce of butter they'd rightfully paid for. When she'd filled the container, she smoothed the top of the butter and pressed the stamp into it. She worked quickly. There was enough butter for five containers, with a little left over to go into a sampler plate, and when she'd stamped the fifth *P* impression, she gathered up the containers and carried them into the gas-run refrigerator in the front of the store.

Paul was showing Timothy how to use a chisel, and he leaned closer to Timothy just as Timothy leaned closer to Paul, and their backs were both straight and their heads angled together. Like a father and a son, she realized, her heart giving a squeeze.

Haddie slipped back into the kitchen, leaving Paul and Timothy alone. She shouldn't even be entertaining such thoughts. A long time ago, when she was a teenager, she'd imagined a scene much like that one with her and Paul together...

But they were both a little wiser now, weren't they? The sound of a chisel against hardwood started up—it was a sound Haddie recognized from her own youth, when her *daet* used to make furniture for the home. Her father had known exactly why it wouldn't work with Paul. She let out a slow breath.

"Haddie?"

She turned to see Paul in the doorway again. He came into the kitchen and the door swung shut behind him. The chiseling sound continued.

"I wonder if you'd—" he began, then the words evaporated. He crossed the kitchen and looked down at her, his dark gaze moving questioningly over her face.

"What?" she asked with a self-conscious laugh.

"Are you okay?" he asked.

"Of course."

"Because you don't seem like it," he said. "Did I do anything to upset you? Or…"

"No, not at all." She reached for the metal bowl she'd used for her orange zest, trying to cover the fact that tears were welling in her eyes. "I'm just—"

Paul put a hand over hers, stopping her movement. "You're just what?"

"I'm being stupidly sentimental," she said and forced a smile.

"You're missing Job," he said.

But for the first time in a long time, she wasn't. "I'm missing a time before Job. I miss being young and having my whole life ahead of me, and the fun we used to have—"

And being picked up for singing by a handsome, young Paul Ebersole…

"You're missing your youth?" he said. "You know, I like you better this way."

"What way?" she asked with a forced laugh. "In my old age?"

"Hardly." He shot her a grin and touched her cheek with the pad of his thumb. "I don't see any wrinkles."

"When I smile, there are plenty," she countered.

"Smile lines don't count." His voice deepened, and he didn't move his hand away from her face. His touch was gentle and purposeful. She longed to lean into his hand, but she wouldn't allow herself that familiarity. She'd been married for fifteen years. She knew how these things worked.

Haddie took a step back. "Paul—"

Paul dropped his hand. "We're both single, Haddie."

"I know," she said. "But hopefully we're both wiser, too."

Paul nodded, and he dropped his gaze. "Can I ask you something?"

"*Yah.* Of course."

"Back when we were teens, you broke things off with me and said we'd never be happy together. What did you see in me that told you that?"

"In you?" She eyed him in disbelief. "Paul, it wasn't about you. It was about me. Back when we were dating, I used to pray every night that *Gott* would make me quieter and more submissive. I wasn't being myself with you—not fully. That wasn't fair to either of us."

"It wasn't me?" he asked. "You didn't sense something…awful in me?"

"Awful?" She shook her head. "Paul, you were a wonderful man who deserved a sweet wife who'd comfort you, and complement you. The thing was, my *daet* sat me down and pointed out that you and I have very different temperaments. He said he knew a couple just like us who'd been quite miserable—not because either the husband or wife were bad, but because they were mismatched. He didn't want me to make that mistake. It was never about you. It was about our personalities."

"Your *daet* saw it?" Paul asked.

"He did. And he knew I wasn't being my honest, open self around you. I'm glad he loved me enough to make sure I married someone I could be myself with."

"I'm sorry if I stopped you from being your true self," he said.

She tapped his shoulder lightly. "That was just an immature young woman trying to be more perfect than she really was. Don't feel bad for that, either."

Paul nodded. "That's a relief."

"How long have you worried about this?" she asked.

"Ever since Leah left."

"For eighteen years?" she breathed. She could see it, then—the loss of confidence he would have endured, the questioning, the agonizing over how he could have done things differently, and her heart nearly broke. He'd been blaming himself all these years for Leah's selfishness? He'd been blaming himself for Haddie calling things off? Of course, his romantic relationships seemed to be failures from his side of things...but it had never been him. She stood up on the tips of her toes and pressed a kiss against his cheek, and his beard tickled her chin. He smelled clean and musky, and her heart gave a little jump at her impetuosity. Had she just kissed him?

Paul looked at her in surprise. "What was that for?"

"You're a better man than you seem to know, Paul," she said.

That kiss was too much—this was always her problem. She galloped over the line over and over again. The bell jingled from the front of the store, and she felt a wave of relief. She didn't need to explain anymore. That was her escape.

"Customers!" she said brightly, and dashed back into the shop.

Chapter Seven

Paul stood there for a moment, feeling the heat hit his face. Haddie had just kissed him…and the soft scents of vanilla and orange hung in the air where she'd stood next to him. Haddie Petersheim didn't seem to notice how beautiful she was, or what kind of effect an innocent kiss like that could have on a man. The spot on his shoulder where she'd laid her hand when she'd pressed that kiss against his cheek still tingled.

He watched the door swing shut after her, her voice filtering back to him from the front of the store as she greeted her customer. She was just a little too cheery, a tad too rushed.

Paul smiled to himself and shook his head. Her words were still ringing in his ears. He hadn't done anything to chase her away. She hadn't seen some awful sign that he'd be a miserable husband... It hadn't been his fault that Haddie had broken things off—she was just trying to be pragmatic about her own personality, and he couldn't fault her for that.

Paul pushed open the swinging door. Haddie stood at the open refrigerator taking out some rolls of butter, and her gaze flickered in his direction. Her cheeks were pink.

Paul hadn't had a woman in his life to give him sympathy or kisses. So maybe that kiss had touched his heart just a little more deeply than it would have for another man who had those gentler influences on his life. He knew it had been a kiss out of sympathy, but he'd still hold on to that memory.

The next day, after his work at the dairy was finished, Paul drove his buggy back down the familiar roads toward Cecily's house. Haddie's story about her father was still fresh in his mind. She and her *daet* had been close enough that he'd been able to tell her when he thought she was making a mistake in her choice of boyfriend, and she hadn't resented him—she'd listened. Haddie's father had had a very strong relationship with his *kinner*, and at this stage of his life, Paul could appreciate that. Maybe he could have a similar relationship with his daughter, given time. Maybe she'd listen to his hard-won wisdom, too.

Dare he hope?

When Paul pulled into Cecily's drive, he saw his daughter sitting outside on the porch, a cell phone in her hands. Her shoulders were stooped, and he could hear Taylor crying from inside. He reined in his horses, wondering why Abigail was outside if her baby was crying in the house.

"Abigail?" he called as he hopped down. "Is everything okay?"

"*Mammi* said I could take a break," Abigail said dully. "She's taking over with Taylor for a bit."

"Oh." The baby's cries were more insistent now, and Abigail looked toward the door, tears in her eyes, too. She was overwhelmed.

"My cell phone is almost out of battery," Abigail said, and she dropped it irritably into her lap. "I hate this! I hate all of it!"

"What, exactly?" Paul asked, worry worming up inside of him.

"This life! What do you people even do? It's so boring! I'm cooped up! My baby just cries nonstop! And I don't have a computer, or TV, or anything!"

"*Yah...*" Paul wasn't sure what to say. "It's different than you're used to. I can see that."

"All I want is to follow my TikTok feed for a few minutes!" Abigail dashed a tear off her cheek. "I can't even do that!"

If she wanted her cell phone in working order, that was something he could take care of for her. If she was an Amish girl, he'd be more reluctant in making this decision, but Abigail wasn't Amish. He could be her solution for this one problem.

"I can charge it for you," Paul said.

"What?" Abigail looked up at him, confused. "I thought you don't have any electricity."

"We do in the barn," Paul said.

"Since when?" she demanded. "I thought that was 'forbidden'!" She used air quotes.

"We don't have electricity in the house," Paul said, "and we only use the electricity in the milking barn for necessary procedures to follow safety regulations set up by the state, but I've got some free outlets if you want me to charge it and bring it back to you later."

"Dad, you're the best!" Abigail said, the words bursting out of her.

Dad. He'd never get tired of hearing her call him that. It might not be the Amish word, but it was beautiful all the same. Abigail looked toward the house again, and for a moment, they both listened to the sound of Taylor's wails. His granddaughter's cries were tugging at his heart, and he couldn't imagine that Abigail was immune to them.

"Do you want to hold your baby?" Paul asked uncertainly.

"I'm no help," Abigail said, her chin quivering. "This is the way she cried and cried when I tried to give her away."

Was she ready to talk about it? Paul leaned against the porch railing and looked up at his daughter. He didn't say anything, just waited.

"Did you know that I did that?" she asked miserably. "I put her on a doorstep and I left. I had a note with her and a bottle, and I just… I left."

"*Yah*, I heard," he said softly.

"So I'm not a good mother," she said.

"You're a very young mother," Paul said gently. "I dare say you still need some mothering, yourself."

Abigail wiped her cheeks with her palms. She felt like this was the end of the world—he could see that as clear as day all over her face. She thought that this moment with her baby crying inside defined who she was as a mother, as a woman… But it didn't. It was just a tough day.

"It's got to be easier with your *mammi* helping you," Paul added.

"Yeah, but she's doing all the hard stuff. I'm not the one Taylor needs."

"Says who?" he asked.

"She's crying, anyway, whether I hold her or not!" Abigail said, turning toward him. "If I was any use, she'd be quiet for me, at least! I hate when she cries like this! It just tears my heart out!"

"The thing with *kinner*—I mean, children—is that they don't know what they need. And they certainly don't make you feel any better about yourself. But they're still yours. And you keep showing up."

Like he was doing. Could she see that he was trying his best to be a father to her?

"I miss Mom." Abigail opened the screen door, and he could feel her pulling away again. He couldn't leave things this way—his daughter feeling desperate, and him feeling helpless.

"Do you want me to take a turn with the baby?" Paul asked suddenly.

Abigail turned back. "You actually want to? *Mammi* says the men play with the happy babies and the women take care of the real work."

Very nice, Cecily, Paul thought to himself, but he said out loud, "That's not the kind of *dawdie* I want to be. I want to help you, Abigail. I want to hold my screaming granddaughter, and walk around the room with her, until she gets so tired that she goes to sleep. I want to take my turn holding a howling baby who I love very much. Is that okay?"

Abigail stared at him in mute surprise for a moment, and then she laughed tearily. "If you really want to."

Paul shot her a smile. "I'm just going to unhitch my horses and I'll be right there. I'll rock her until one of us passes out—that's a promise."

And it seemed to him that his daughter's shoulders relaxed just a little bit more at his goofy humor. He hadn't expected to come be on baby duty, but he was glad to do it. He'd never held Abigail as a baby, but he could hold her daughter. And no amount of screaming and crying was going to chase him off from being a father and grandfather at long last.

Cecily's estimation of men was dead wrong.

Haddie reined the horse in at the four-way stop and waited while a car passed the other way. Then she flicked the reins again and her buggy rattled forward. She missed Job most of all for appointments like this one. If Job was alive, he'd still be running the shop while she visited the teacher, and when she got back and told him the news, he'd sit their son down for a serious talk. She wouldn't be handling this on her own, like she was today.

And Haddie wasn't handling things as well as she wanted everyone to believe. Her son was getting into trouble, and apparently, Haddie was overstepping all polite boundary lines in kissing Paul's cheek! What had she been thinking? Her face grew hot at the memory.

They hadn't spoken about it, either. Yesterday, Haddie had served some customers, and Paul had finished up with Timothy for the afternoon, and then gone home. He'd said a cordial goodbye.

And that was it. He'd dropped off the cream this morning, but he hadn't stayed, and she'd been carrying around her embarrassment all day.

She was the one trying to teach Timothy how to act appropriately! He'd gotten his impetuous nature from her. Because as in control as she was now as a grown woman, she'd been a girl who acted out when she was upset about things, too.

And here, she'd brazenly kissed a man on the cheek all because she was feeling a jumble of emotions surrounding him… What was wrong with her?

The school was coming up ahead. The sound of children's laughter surfed on the icy breeze, and she could make out the squeaking from the swing set. The children had dug out a path to let them swing. Would Timothy be playing with the others? He knew she was coming for a meeting with the teacher this afternoon, and she deeply hoped she'd find him playing tag, or making snowballs, acting like every other happy boy his age. But as she steered the horse into the school's buggy parking lot, she spotted her son sitting alone on the front steps, his schoolbag beside him. He was looking morosely in her direction, his gaze following the buggy as she reined in the horses.

"Oh, Timothy…" she breathed.

Timothy stood and came slowly in her direction, and Haddie hopped down, rubbing her cold, gloved hands together. She got the feed bag from the back of the buggy, and when Timothy arrived at her side, she handed it to him. He knew what to do, and while he silently went about it, she got out the horse blanket.

"What will your teacher tell me?" Haddie asked Timothy as she tossed the blanket over the horse's back.

"I dunno." Timothy dug his boot into the snowy ground.

While she'd rather hear from him first, she'd find out soon enough. Haddie put a hand on his shoulder and looked down into his face.

"Timothy, I love you," she said. "And I know you're a good boy."

Deep, deep down, past the shenanigans, her son had a very good heart. Timothy looked less convinced, and they walked together up toward the schoolhouse, past the laughing, playing children. Some of the children stopped to look at them—a group of three girls whispering together, and Josh Ebersole's son, Simon, standing in the snow beside the swing set, staring at them intently. Haddie refused to look at any of them. Doubtlessly, they knew what her son had done to garner this meeting.

Betty Beiler opened the door and beckoned them inside with a smile. She was a tall, thin woman in her sixties.

"Good afternoon, Haddie," Betty said. "I'm sorry to pull you away from the shop. I know it's not convenient."

Haddie didn't have any other employees to take over for her, either, so she'd simply put up a sign that she was running an errand and would reopen the next day. Here was hoping she didn't lose too many sales, because they needed every customer they could get.

"It's all right," Haddie said, and she nudged her son into the schoolhouse ahead of her.

The school was warm inside, a potbellied stove in the middle of the room cheerily pump-

ing heat. The blackboard had been cleaned off
with a wet cloth, leaving behind some rect-
angles on the top of the board that included
homework assignments for different grades.
Betty led them inside, and waited while Haddie pulled off her gloves before she gestured to
a few chairs she'd arranged next to the stove.

"I'm glad you could come today," Betty
said. "I've talked to Timothy several times,
myself, and I'm just not seeing the changes I
need to see in his behavior."

Betty looked pointedly down at Timothy,
who squirmed.

"What is he doing?" Haddie asked.

"He's talking during class," Betty said, "and
he's teasing the girls every chance he gets. He
won't pay attention during class time, and he
draws pictures in his notebook instead, which
means he's missing out on important learning."

Haddie sighed.

"This is new this year," Betty went on. "He
was my star pupil last year—weren't you,
Timothy? You used to work hard, and you
were polite and respectful. I was very proud
of you, especially since it was a very difficult
year for you."

The year after his father's death. It had been
a difficult year for both of them.

"I'll talk with him," Haddie said. What else could she do?

"It's not just the disruptive behavior," Betty went on. "He's been disappearing during lunch hours, and no one is to leave school property without permission. But he runs off, and sometimes it's halfway through the first class after lunch before he comes back."

"You run away?" Haddie turned toward Timothy, alarmed. "Where do you go?"

"Just for a walk," Timothy said.

"It's dangerous," Haddie said. "You don't just walk the back roads during lunch. You eat your food and play with your friends."

"I don't want to play with them," Timothy said.

"Do you have anyone to play with?" Haddie asked, lowering her voice.

"*Yah*, of course!" Timothy replied. "I just don't want to, so I go for a walk."

"Well, stop it," Haddie retorted. "Anything could happen, and we'd never know where to start looking. When you're at school, you stay on school property. Period."

"Okay." Timothy's voice was low.

So she'd had to shut down the shop and come out here for a meeting for this? She'd have to discipline Timothy somehow, but she wasn't sure what would get through to him. He never was an easy child to raise.

"I'm sorry about all of this," Haddie said, turning back to the teacher. "Believe me, we talk about respect and cooperation at home. And we'll talk about it a whole lot more. I don't know what has gotten into him."

Betty looked down at the ash bucket next to her and frowned.

"Timothy, I forgot to assign someone to empty this," she said, lifting it up. "Would you take care of that for me?"

"Okay," Timothy said, and accepted the bucket from her hands, then headed slowly toward the door.

"Hurry now!" Betty called. "Your mother has things to do, I'm sure!" Timothy disappeared outside, and Betty sighed. "That's better. Now, I'll say this quickly because he'll be back soon enough. He lost his *daet*, and that just broke his little heart. I have grandchildren his age, and I know how important that relationship with a father is to a little boy. I think it might be as simple as having some men he can spend time with."

Haddie pressed her lips together. It wasn't anyone's business, but that wasn't quite so easy. They had the creamery to run, and a home to keep up.

"I hope I haven't offended you," Betty added.

"No, you haven't," Haddie said. "I know this has been very hard for him. I'll see what I can do. As for the bench, he's working with Paul Ebersole to build you a new one. It'll be replaced, and Timothy is really working hard on it."

"I'm glad to hear it," Betty said with a sympathetic smile. "Paul's a good man, and I'm glad he was willing to help you. Maybe more time with Paul might be good for Timothy."

Haddie wouldn't answer that. Things with Paul were complicated enough as it was, and she couldn't put the raising of her son onto other people's shoulders. She believed in their community, but she also believed in raising her own child.

"Let me know how things go," Haddie said.

The door opened and Timothy came back inside, his cheeks pink from the cold. He put the ash bin down by the door.

"We're ready to go," Haddie said, and she met her son at the door. She turned back to give Betty one last nod, then nudged her son out the door.

"You and I need to talk, young man," she said, and Timothy shuffled off toward the buggy.

This lecture would be a long one, and she

had so many things to say, she wasn't even sure where to start.

Gott, *give me the words*, she prayed, *because I don't know how to get through to him!*

Chapter Eight

The next morning, before Petersheim Creamery opened, Paul tipped a finished display shelf into place along the wall. It was tall and sturdy, and felt smooth under his fingertips. He was proud of his work. He'd give Haddie a beautiful shop, and maybe in the future she'd remember him as she looked over the details, like the perfectly square corners, the tight seams and the meticulously installed anchors to hold the shelves against the walls no matter what got into old Barnabas's mind.

Did women notice those things? He hoped so, because that was how a man showed that he cared—it was in the silent details.

Barnabas was lying by the door to the kitchen in his usual spot, and Haddie was at the open refrigerator, putting newly packaged butter onto the shelves. Outside, the temperature hovered just above freezing, and while the road and sidewalks were clear, a frigid sleet was coming down from the sky, splattering against the windows and making him grateful for the woodstove heat.

"So where does Timothy go?" Paul asked, picking up on the conversation they'd started earlier that morning. Haddie had been telling him about the meeting with the teacher, and Paul's mind was stuck on Timothy leaving the school during his lunch hour. Where would a boy go in the middle of the day by himself?

"I don't know," she replied, her voice muffled as she leaned into the fridge. "But I had a very long talk with him on the ride home."

"What did you say to him?" he asked.

"Oh..." Haddie closed the fridge door and turned back toward him. "Everything... I told him that I know how hard these last couple of years have been, but that doesn't give us an excuse to do dangerous things, or cause damage. We have to talk about our feelings."

"That sounds reasonable," Paul replied.

"I don't know..." She sighed. "He's ten. What sounds reasonable to a man in his forties is entirely different than what makes sense to a child's brain."

Paul looked over to the half-finished bench

that Timothy had been working on. He was doing a decent job of it, too.

"He gets it from me, you know," Haddie added.

"What?" Paul eyed her curiously. Timothy had his mother's dark eyes and long lashes— that was something he'd noticed between mother and son.

"His impetuous nature," Haddie replied. "I was always into some sort of trouble at his age."

"I don't believe that," Paul said with a chuckle.

"I broke a window in our house playing baseball with my brothers in the garden," she said.

"I'd blame your brothers," he said with a grin.

"I ate an entire row of my mother's cherry jam from the pantry—about seven jars over the course of a week," she said, and her eyes glittered at the memory.

"It must have been good jam," he said. "And your mother must have been furious."

"She was. I had to help make a whole new batch of jam, and she made me do all the dishes, too," Haddie replied. "Do you know how many dishes are involved in making jam?"

"You were a kid," he said.

"I was a rascal," she replied. "I used to tell my aunts and uncles when my parents would have disagreements behind closed doors that they tried to hide from us *kinner*. I'd tell them details, too."

"Oh, Haddie, that's terrible!" But Paul couldn't help but laugh. "You really were a handful! Why?"

"I don't know," she said. "Some little girls are quiet and want to please people. I wasn't very good at sitting still and behaving myself. I wasn't any good at keeping my mouth shut, either. And indulging my impulses was more satisfying than it was to make other people happy with me."

"Have you outgrown it?" he asked jokingly.

"Not entirely." She wasn't joking. "What about you? Were you a good child or a rambunctious one?"

Paul wished he had some stories about horrible things he'd done as a boy to match hers—it would comfort her, he could tell—but he didn't have too many of them.

"I peeked at my birthday gift once," he said.

"What happened?" she asked.

"Nothing. I just knew that my parents were giving me a scooter. That's all." Paul shrugged.

"And a few times I used bad words and my *mamm* washed my mouth out with soap."

"Anything more dramatic than that?" she asked hopefully.

Paul laughed softly. "I was a pretty calm kid. Maybe that's why I was attracted to girls with more spunk."

Haddie met his gaze thoughtfully. "You need to watch that tendency in yourself, Paul Ebersole."

He felt the gentle remonstrance in her words. Did her father have a point in his way of always being drawn to women who challenged him? He had to admit, he didn't want a home with arguments and disagreements all the time. He wanted a peaceful, happy home at the end of a long day of hard work. He wanted a hot meal and warm smiles. He and Leah had never managed to get a home like that. They'd argued too much.

"I probably do," he admitted.

But a man couldn't help the kinds of women who sparked his interest, could he? Was it even fair to marry a woman who left him feeling lukewarm?

"Could you help me with something?" Paul asked. He hoisted the second finished shelf onto its side. "I need you help me stabilize it while I get it anchored to the wall."

"Of course."

Haddie came over, and Paul stifled a grunt while he lifted the shelf upright. It was solid wood, and heavy, and he caught Haddie's gaze move down to his biceps. He carried the bulk of the shelf's weight on his own, and truth be told, he was showing off just a little bit.

"Careful," Haddie said. "That's very heavy."

"Nah," he said. "I've got it."

He grimaced as he lifted the shelf into place. On the back he had some treated canvas strips that he would use to anchor the shelf to a stud in the wall.

"Can you hold it right here?" he asked, keeping the shelf tipped slightly forward to give him space to work behind it.

Haddie moved toward him, but she wasn't quite in the right position. He put an arm around her shoulders and tugged her in closer. She smelled nice, he noticed—like freshly laundered clothes and something soft and floral.

"Don't be shy," he said with a low laugh. "You'll be able to hold it better from here."

He dropped his hand and leaned back behind the bookcase to screw the strap against the wall.

"So tell me more about your childhood adventures," he said.

He felt the shelf shake as she laughed. "I became vegetarian for three weeks when I was thirteen."

"What?" He pulled back out to look at her. "I don't think I've ever heard of an Amish vegetarian, unless you count old Thomas Esh, who had to go off meat because of his heart condition. But he still ate fish."

"I was making a point because I was attached to this little flock of chickens," she said. "I'd raised them from chicks, and they would come running to me to be pet. I loved them so much. My parents had warned me not to make them into pets because we were raising them for eggs and meat."

Paul went back behind the shelf with his screwdriver, biting his lip as he stretched to reach the screw. The angle was awkward, but he was able to get the screw into the hole he'd hand-drilled into the stud, his forearm burning with the effort of driving the screw into the wood.

"My brother told me that I couldn't play favorites. If I ate beef and pork, then it was just the same," Haddie went on. "So I declared myself a vegetarian."

"For three weeks," Paul said.

"Yes."

"You just got hungry after that?" he asked.

"I got more than hungry. I started to actually shake. It turns out potatoes and string beans aren't enough nutrition for a growing girl. My mother saw my hands trembling, sat me down and gave me a piece of leftover meatloaf. I can't remember anything tasting so good."

Paul laughed, imagining the indignant Haddie bent on making her point. At least her parents had loved her enough to make sure she started eating properly again. He wondered if his own daughter would be this much of a challenge.

"How did I not know any of this?" he asked.

"When you and I were getting to know each other, I was too busy trying to be someone better," she replied. "I wouldn't have told you any of these stories. Every time I saw you, I'd count the number of times I talked to make sure I talked less."

Outside, the wind moaned and the sleet pattered steadily against the windowpane. He looked at her quizzically. Was she joking again? She'd been stopping herself from talking with him? That was a terrible thought. Paul eased the now-secured shelf back against the wall, and as he turned, he found himself so close to Haddie that he could feel her breath.

"You really weren't being yourself with me?" he asked quietly.

"No, I wasn't," she said. "I was being the model of a nice young woman who wanted to get married."

"Did I make you feel like you needed to change yourself?" he asked. "That's awful."

"No, it wasn't you. It was… We girls were told what a young man wanted in a wife. And you were no different than any other young man. I just wanted to be that kind of woman. And I tried my best, but changing your personality isn't actually possible."

"Some of our time together was honest, though," he pressed. "The laughter, the long drives where we'd look up at the stars. You told me a lot about yourself when I took you out. Don't tell me you were lying."

"I was telling the truth," she said. "But not all of it. Like I said, I was trying to be a certain type of woman, and a lot of my childhood stories didn't match with that. So I wasn't lying, but I was certainly editing what I told you. The whole picture is important, wouldn't you say?"

"*Yah*, of course," he said. "I would have liked to hear these stories about when you were little, though."

Haddie smiled faintly. "You find it all funny and entertaining because there is no worry that your future children will end up like me. These stories are well and good between friends, but when people are courting, they're a little more careful."

She'd been hiding her true self from him, and that made him feel a wave of sadness.

"You didn't trust that I'd like the real you?" he asked.

"My *daet* set me straight," she replied. "He said that I couldn't hold my breath for the rest of my life, and that a man would have some serious regrets if he married a girl thinking he was getting one type of person and got someone completely different."

"Are you being your honest self now?" he asked.

"Of course. I'm no longer a girl. I'm a widow. I'm a mother. I have nothing left to pretend, Paul."

He felt a wave of relief. He didn't want her to pretend with him. He didn't want her to feel like she had to walk on eggshells with him. He'd worried for eighteen years that he'd been the problem, and he wasn't going to start being one now.

"Good." Paul's voice caught, and he reached out and moved a stray hair off her cheek. He wasn't even sure why he did it, except that he felt tenderness welling up inside of him. As his fingers brushed her soft cheek, her lips parted, and something in the moment suddenly deepened.

He hadn't kissed a woman since his marriage. And before that—twenty years ago—it had been Haddie he'd shared some kisses with in his courting buggy. He was a man who'd lived a single life, and he didn't know if he would still have the knack for it, but looking at her pink lips, he couldn't think of anything else. He ran his thumb across her chin, and his heartbeat hammered in his ears. When she didn't move back, he leaned in and touched her lips with his.

The kiss was gentle and cautious at first, but then she leaned toward him, her hand resting on the center of his chest, and all of his hesitation fell away. He might not know how to kiss a woman anymore, but he certainly seemed to know how to kiss *her*. He slid his arms around her waist and tugged her in closer.

This kiss had taken him by surprise, but it was also a strange relief. It explained what he'd been feeling toward Haddie these last few days, the building protectiveness he'd been experiencing. Everything was culminating in this kiss.

Haddie pulled back, her cheeks flushed. The

sound of wet snow slapped the window behind him, and he gave her a half smile.

"I've been thinking about that for a while," he said.

"I noticed that." Her cheeks turned pinker.

So he hadn't been hiding that as well as he'd hoped. She'd been in a marriage longer than he had, so maybe it was silly of him to hope for some face-saving naivety from her.

"You aren't going to pretend you didn't?" he asked hopefully. "It might help me save face."

"I'm hopelessly honest now," she said with a faint shrug.

What was it about this woman that tugged him in like this? Of course, she was all wrong for him…but Haddie was confusingly endearing. And her frank gaze pulled him in in spite of himself.

"Should I apologize for kissing you?" he whispered.

A smile tickled her lips. "No. I don't think so. It was…nice."

"Really?" His heart gave a little leap in surprise. She'd enjoyed the kiss, too…

"It's been so long since I've been kissed." Her cheeks turned pinker. "But we should be careful from now on. I think we're both old enough to know not to play with this, right?"

"Yah." That was the sobering thought he

needed. They weren't young people, naively following their feelings. "But for the record, Haddie, I do think you're beautiful."

She dropped her gaze. "Paul…"

"I just wanted to say it," he said. "I'm not asking for more."

There was a beat of silence, and then Haddie said, "I think you're very good-looking, too, Paul."

His chest swelled at that comment, and he tried to catch her gaze, but she looked down.

"I'd better open up the store," she said.

They both looked toward the window, and there was no one waiting, just that steady, driving sleet. If only there had been some customers to distract them from the awkwardness of the moment.

"Yah," he said. "Of course. I've got to get started on the next shelf."

But as he watched her bustle up to the front door and flip the sign in the window to Open, he couldn't help but smile to himself.

Paul shouldn't have kissed her, but he wasn't sorry for it, either. He'd forgotten all the sweet little details of life with a woman he'd missed out on these last eighteen years, and Haddie Petersheim was a very good reminder. She was soft and pretty, but also as strong as hardwood. She was a confusing mix of elements that he couldn't quite sweep from his mind when he went home after a day here working on her shop.

He wouldn't kiss her again—he had to be sure before he started a proper romance, and neither of them were sure. That was clear. He couldn't afford to make any mistakes this time around, but he was tucking away this memory, all the same.

The kiss had been wonderful.

Haddie worked on a new batch of butter in the back kitchen between customers that day, and for the most part, Paul stayed hard at work on those shelves. He went out for lunch, and offered to take her with him, but she turned him down. More time together wasn't going to be a good thing…at least not for her. That kiss was seared into her mind, and she couldn't seem to stop thinking about what it felt like to be pulled in close, his lips covering hers, his beard tickling her face…

She pushed back the thought.

Barnabas was a traitor and went to lie down close to where Paul was working. He'd always preferred Job to her, too. Barnabas must miss having a man around. Maybe she did, too, because it was oddly soothing to listen to the shushing of the sandpaper and the reverberation of his deep voice when he talked to the dog.

She'd gotten used to being alone in the shop during the days—she'd even gotten to like it. But this time with Paul reminded her of sweeter days, when her husband had been in the shop with her and they'd work in companionable silence, or talk about the latest news in the local *Budget* paper. A man in the room even changed the scent of the place, and it was more than comforting—it made her feel a little more alive.

Haddie missed a husband's warm smile. She missed being kissed—was that terrible to admit? Because she did! She missed being able to simply walk up to a husband and lean into his arms—no hesitation. She missed making a man happy just by being there, and having a man think she made the room prettier because she was in it. Not that Paul had said that, exactly, but his kiss had woken up a part of her that should have remained dormant.

Haddie missed being married.

So when Paul got back with a take-out container of French fries for her after his lunch break, she'd been touched that he'd gone to the trouble, but she still tried to keep herself busy.

The hours slipped by and the weather improved. The sloppy, wet sleet turned into proper snow, and then the sky cleared up and the sun peeked through, sending some welcome beams through the front window. With the improved weather came more customers, and Haddie sold most of her butter. Paul nearly finished another shelf by the time Timothy was due to come home after school. She kept an eye on the road, waiting for the Lapp buggy.

The store was starting to come together. Four completed shelves, sanded and oiled to perfection, now lined the walls. The shelves were taller than before, and there was more room for merchandise. She was already wondering what she might put in there—maybe crafts from some local women? Those were always popular with the tourists. Paul was doing a good job, and she watched as he picked up a few scraps of wood from the floor and tossed them into a cardboard box.

"Haddie," Paul said, his voice low.

"Yah?"

"Did I ruin things with us?" he asked. "We were getting to be friends, and I really valued that. I probably shouldn't have crossed that line."

"We've both been putting off getting married," Haddie said. "Maybe it's time you found that sweet, young bride, and I found my older, affectionate second husband. We've been spending time together, and getting to be good friends, and I think it's natural that two adults might...trip over the line."

"Two of us tripped?" he asked.

"Yah..." She had kissed him back, after all.

"I never had much romance of my own," Paul said.

"But you deserve it, Paul," she said. "And you deserve another chance at the kind of marriage you always wanted."

"Is it as nice as it looks from the outside?" he asked.

Haddie nodded, her eyes misting. "It really is. The sun is brighter, the stove is warmer and you have someone to take care of. It's worth finding your perfect wife, Paul."

A buggy rattled past, and she looked out to see that it wasn't Miriam Lapp with the boys. She didn't have much time until Timothy got here, though, and they certainly couldn't talk about this in front of him. So she'd have to get to the point.

"Maybe that kiss was actually for the best," she said hopefully. "It jostled us both out of our comfortable routines. It reminded us of what we're missing out on."

A memory of that kiss was stamped into her

mind, and her heart sped up at the memory. But he wasn't hers to kiss.

"It's different now that we're older," she went on. "We can think about these things more rationally."

Except, it hadn't been all that different from when she was younger. She still felt like that kiss was going to occupy her thoughts for a good long while…but it *should* be different. And it could be if she put her mind to it.

Paul shot her an acknowledging look, but didn't say anything. Was she convincing him, at least?

"I'm going to have to go to the farm-supply store," Paul said. "I need a couple more brackets to hold up the shelves, and that's where I found the ones I like last time. And that will finish up this shelf."

Back to practical concerns. It did sting a little that he hadn't argued more, and she wondered if she'd hurt his feelings.

"It really is looking nice, Paul," she said, swallowing hard.

"I'm glad you like it."

Another buggy and hooves sounded outside, and this time when Haddie looked out the window, she saw Miriam reining in in front of the shop. It was good that Timothy was home. She needed the buffer zone. Timothy hopped out of the back and waved to the boys she couldn't see. Haddie opened the front door to wave at Miriam.

Across the room, Paul was putting his tools back into the box, getting ready to go to the store. Maybe he'd be glad to get away from her for a few minutes. She wouldn't blame him.

"How was your day at school?" Haddie asked as Timothy came through the door.

Her son shrugged out of his backpack. "It was okay."

"Do you have homework?"

"Yeah, a bit."

"Are there any letters from the teacher today?" she asked.

"No!" Timothy shot her an annoyed look. "But my boots are too small."

"What?" she looked down at his feet. "I just bought you those." She bent down and felt the toe of his boot. "Wiggle."

Timothy obediently wiggled his toes, and sure enough, they were at the very end of the boots. He was growing so quickly lately!

Paul took off his work gloves and slapped them against his thigh. "Growing without permission again?" he joked.

Timothy shot Paul a grin. "Oops."

"Are you ready to finish up that bench this afternoon?" Paul asked.

"Will we finish it?" Timothy asked.

"*Yah.* If you work hard." Paul turned to Haddie. "I'm heading to the shop, anyway, so I can take him for boots, if you want."

No, that definitely felt a little too familiar. After that kiss, everything was feeling a bit too familiar. It was too easy to start relying on Paul. He was kind, handsome, warm and he had a musky scent about him that made her want to lean a bit closer. No, no, it was far too easy to start leaning on Paul in a way that wouldn't be right. She'd buy his boots herself.

"It's okay, I'll do it." Haddie picked up a sign that read Be Back in a Jiffy and replaced the Open sign with it. "Timothy, go put your bag in the back, and then we'll leave."

"I get new boots?" Timothy asked, brightening.

"*Yah,* you'll get new boots. You can't go squeezing into those for much longer."

"Thanks, *Mamm!*"

Timothy disappeared through the swinging doors into the kitchen, and Haddie cast Paul a smile.

"But thank you for the offer," she said.

"I'll wait for you, then," Paul said. "We might as well walk over together."

Chapter Nine

Redemption's Farm Supply was a rural community's response to Walmart. Amish folk did hire vans to take them into the city to shop at big-box stores, but that was a rare treat, and most times when people needed something, they headed down to the farm supply, where they could find everything from winter boots and snow pants to dishes, cattle ear tags and bovine medication. It was a farming retail catchall for the locals' needs.

Redemption's Farm Supply was located at the far end of Main Street, just past the leather-and-tack shop. Paul held the door open for Haddie and Timothy to go inside ahead of him, and an *Englisher* family with parents and two children passed them on their way out of the shop. The man gave Paul a nod.

It was the kind of male nod that men exchanged when they acknowledged another man in a similar circumstance, the way men in rain boots would nod at each other in the city, or Amish men would acknowledge each other at an auction.

It took Paul a moment to register what he had in common with that man besides gender, but then it struck him. Paul looked like he was out with his family, too. With his married beard, a beautiful woman at his side and a boy along with them, they certainly looked the part. He felt a strange rush of protectiveness. Haddie might not be his, but he did want to make sure she was okay. He did want to help.

Timothy went ahead of them down the center aisle, past the milking supplies, bovine supplements, some kitchen bakeware and a rack of safety coats with reflective tape. He stopped at a little display of yellow leather tool belts. They were in children's sizes, and they were loaded full of tools about three quarters the size of regular tools, with a hammer, a chisel, a couple of screwdrivers and an adjustable wrench. They caught Paul's eye, too, truthfully.

"Mamm?" Timothy turned toward his mother, his eyes bright.

Paul knew that look. He'd felt that same awe and longing himself as a boy countless

times when he'd walked with his *daet* through
a farm-supply store. There was always something to catch a boy's eye and fill his heart
with desire.

"No, Timothy. We're here for boots," Haddie said.

Timothy didn't move on, though. He reached
out and fingered the tough leather, then pushed
the wrench out, fiddling with the knob that adjusted the grip.

"Timothy, put it back," Haddie said quietly.
"We are here for boots. That's all."

Paul watched as Timothy reluctantly replaced the wrench. The tool belt was actually priced quite well. Paul picked one up and
turned it over in his hands. The tools were
perfect for a child's grip, and the belt was professional quality.

"Those just came in!" Albert Wise, the store
manager called over to him. "Only a few of
them, too. Once they're sold out, they're gone."

That was good to know, and he looked over
at Haddie. Her gaze moved over the tools, and
he thought he saw a flicker of longing in her
eyes, too, at that tool belt. He raised his eyebrows in silent question, but she shook her
head quickly.

"Come along, Timothy," she said. "What

size are your feet now, I wonder. Let's try some on."

Paul found the brackets he was looking for. Down the opposite aisle, Haddie was crouching on the floor, feeling Timothy's toes through a pair of boots.

"How do these feel?" Her voice carried over to where Paul stood.

"Good, I guess."

"I don't like the quality for these ones. That stitching is going to leak water. Take them off."

Paul crossed his arms, watching the pair shop. Timothy looked up at Paul, a smile tickling the corners of his lips. Haddie put back those boots and reached for another pair. She checked the price, hesitated, then put them back and reached for a different style.

She can't afford the tool belt, he realized in a rush. She was raising a growing boy on her own, running a business that her husband used to manage and finding a way to pay all her bills. She had a confident way about her that made her seem just fine no matter what, but she'd burst into tears when those shelves broke. How much pressure was she under these days?

"Try these." Haddie brought down another pair.

"I don't like those." Timothy's attention was back on his mother.

"Why not?"

"They look dumb."

"They're boots!"

"They still look dumb. I like those other ones."

"Those cost far more than boots should cost," she said. "We aren't getting those."

Paul turned away, and headed back up toward the till. As he passed the tool belts, he grabbed one. Timothy might end up with boots he didn't like, but he'd make sure the boy got his tools. Maybe he could use these for finishing the bench, too. It would add to the boy's sense of personal satisfaction if he'd used his own tools for the job.

"Hi, Paul," Albert said. "How's the farm?"

"It's surviving." Paul put the brackets and tool belt on the counter. "How're Sarah and the girls?"

"Tabitha has a terrible cold right now," Albert replied. "It's just hanging on and won't quit."

"Oh, I'm sorry."

"But she's on the mend." He scanned the items and put them into a plastic bag. "Those tool belts were a great find. I saw them at a tool show in Baltimore, and I knew then that as soon as they hit the catalog, I'd order some in."

"Yah..." Paul lowered his voice. "But I mean it as a surprise."

"Oops." Albert grinned. "We could use another wedding these days, you know. Sarah is embroidering on some dish towels for the next couple to tie the knot."

Paul chuckled. "No, no, it's nothing like that. Those dish towels will go to someone else."

"I hadn't considered a match between the two of you before," Albert said, lowering his voice further. "But now that I think of it, I don't know why it never occurred to me."

"We're friends," Paul said. "That's all."

"Well..." Albert nodded toward the total, and Paul handed over the cash from his wallet.

Haddie and Timothy came down the center aisle then, a pair of boots under Timothy's arm. Haddie's cheeks were slightly pink, and Paul noticed that she'd selected the boots that were too expensive, after all, and he wished there was a way he could help ease her burdens a little more without crossing lines.

If he hadn't kissed her, this would be easier—his declaration of simple friendship would be easy to defend. But if he offered to do too much now, she'd think he was trying to court her, and it would upset an already precarious balance between them.

Timothy looked longingly at the tool belt as they passed, and he reached out to touch the leather once more.

"We talked about this, Timothy." Haddie tapped his shoulder and he dropped his hand. "You know why."

The boy met his mother's gaze, then straightened just a little bit and nodded. He'd have to understand that things were tight, Paul realized. How could he not? They approached the counter, and Paul waited while Haddie paid. As she counted out the bills and reached into the waistband of her apron to pull out a few more, Timothy's gaze fell on Paul's plastic bag.

It was a thin, white plastic, and it didn't exactly hide what was inside. The boy's eyes widened, and his gaze snapped up to Paul's face.

Paul stifled a smile and touched his lips. Timothy nodded, and turned back to face the same direction as his mother, his ears flaming red.

Timothy knew he'd get the tool belt now, and Paul felt a rush of tenderness for the boy. He wasn't a bad boy, but grief wasn't easy to navigate for adults, let alone for *kinner*.

When Haddie had paid, they headed onto the sidewalk again, and Timothy's gaze kept moving back to the bag in Paul's hand.

"Haddie—"

She tugged her shawl a little closer around her shoulders and looked up at him.

"I know you weren't going to get one of those little tool belts, but they're a very good deal, and they'll sell out fast. Albert said that once they're gone, they're gone," he said.

"Not today, Paul," she said firmly.

"I bought one," he said, and he shot her a smile. "I just thought that Timothy would like it."

He pulled it out of the bag and handed it over to Timothy, who received it with a grin and said exuberantly, "Thank you, Paul!"

Haddie's eyes widened, but it wasn't from happiness or pleasure. Her cheeks paled and she pressed her lips together.

"Give it to me," Haddie said, holding her hand out.

"But, *Mamm*—"

"Give it to me," she repeated. Timothy handed it over and she held it out to Paul.

"Haddie…" he said gently.

"Timothy, go on back to our shop," she said. "And I want you to start on your homework right away."

Timothy looked at the tool belt still in his mother's hand, and she thrust it more firmly toward Paul. He reluctantly took it back.

"Now, Timothy!" she said, and the boy took off at a jog down the street. They watched him for a couple of beats, and then Haddie turned back toward him.

"I had said no, Paul," she said. "Why did you do that?"

"I know it's been hard for you, and I thought you'd be happy," Paul said.

"I'm not!" she retorted. "What were you thinking?"

"I was thinking that he's been through a lot, and he wanted some tools. He could use them on that bench. I was thinking that he'd feel some personal pride in work done with his own tools."

Haddie pressed her lips together and she exhaled a shaky breath.

"I am his mother," she said, her voice low. "It is up to me whether he gets something new or not, and you had no right to give it to him without my permission."

"Haddie, I can tell that things are tight right now," he said, stepping closer so they could keep their voices down. "That isn't your fault! But prices keep going up and you're on your own—"

"I don't need charity!" Her eyes flashed fire.

"Charity?" He shook his head. "That wasn't charity, although I should point out that an

Amish community is based on us taking care of each other! And you're a widow, Haddie Petersheim! That makes you all of our responsibility."

She shook her head and cast a scathing look out at the street, making a passing *Englisher* man jump.

"How about a gift from someone who cares?" Paul asked.

Haddie spun on her heels and started down the street, and Paul caught up with her in a few brisk steps. His heart was hammering hard in his chest, because this felt all too familiar—not with any argument he'd ever had with Haddie, but with the fights he'd had with Leah early in their marriage.

He seemed to be missing out on what was upsetting her and had only made it worse.

"Haddie," he whispered loudly next to her. "What did I do wrong?"

"You are not his *daet*!" A tear escaped her lashes and she dashed it off her cheek.

"I know..." That stung, because he wasn't trying to be the boy's father.

So that was what this was about? She was protective of Job's memory? *Yah*, he wasn't Timothy's father, but he was a man who cared. And Timothy needed that right now, *daet* or not. But he felt his heart falter and sink back.

"He's been getting into trouble at school!" Her voice was tight, and he saw tears shine in her eyes. "He's been breaking furniture, for crying out loud! He's been disappearing at lunch hours. I am not rewarding that kind of behavior! When I said no, I meant it. And I had good reason! I knew what I was doing, and now my son is left with the impression that he'll still get what he wants if he has a kind friend. And I'm now the cruel mother who dashes his happiness instead of the loving mother who is teaching him how to behave!"

"Haddie, I didn't mean to get in the way of your raising him," Paul said. "I'm sorry."

She was still angry, he could tell. Her cache of emotion hadn't been spent yet, but his had. He eyed her uncertainly. And then she deflated—all at once.

"I am sorry," he repeated.

"Paul, this all felt a little too—" she shrugged "—family-like."

"I see," he murmured.

"Our time together, our..." Her cheeks pinked even more than they were from the cold. "Our kiss, even. It all reminds me a little too much of married life."

Right. He had felt some of that, too, but he'd enjoyed it. Apparently, it wasn't quite so pleasant for her.

"And then having you give a gift like that to Timothy—it isn't just that I was telling him no for a reason. It's also that it feels too close." Haddie sucked in a breath, and she fell silent as two *Englisher* women passed them on the sidewalk.

"I'm not used to this," Paul admitted. "I've just been an uncle for so long, that now that I'm a *daet* to Abigail, it's opening up a different side to me, and... I guess I got enthusiastic."

Haddie swallowed. "Timothy is getting attached to you, Paul, and I don't want to break his heart."

"He is?" What did it say about him that he was rather gratified to hear it? His own daughter was having a tougher time getting comfortable around him, but he and Timothy seemed to connect.

"He is," she said, and she didn't sound pleased about that. "He talks about you at home a lot. Before I tucked him in last night, he said that your nephew Simon always talks about doing things with his *daet*, and he gets so jealous of him. But now that he's making a bench with you, he doesn't feel so jealous anymore."

"So I'm helping," Paul said.

"You are, but maybe too much. Hard times

need to be softened for children, I agree, but we also have to learn to accept facts, and deal with our feelings. My son is no different. He has to learn to be grateful for what he has. And he's not on his own."

"He needs to be grateful for *you*," Paul murmured.

"It would be nice." Her voice shook, but she picked up her pace.

"Do you still want me to help him finish that bench?" he asked. "Or should I…let someone else?"

"If you'd help him, I'd be very grateful," she said, "but keep all of this in mind. Timothy wants a father—a real one. And it's better to have his hopes let down now than later."

Kinner weren't quite so simple to deal with, after all. If it was just about what made the boy happy, Paul could easily supply that. But what about what Timothy needed in the long run? That was his mother's job to anticipate.

And maybe he'd upended Haddie's careful balance, too. He shouldn't have kissed her.

For the first time since pulling her into his arms, he felt regret.

He wouldn't be doing that again.

Haddie kept Petersheim Creamery open a little bit later that evening since customers were still coming in, and Paul and Timothy were still working on that bench. By the time she flipped the window sign to Closed, Paul had helped Timothy pound in the last wooden peg with a mallet to keep the bench together.

"It looks good," Haddie said.

"*Yah*, it does. Better than the one I broke," Timothy said.

"Although that one shouldn't have been broken," Haddie added.

"I know, *Mamm*."

Haddie met Paul's gaze, and she read some sadness there. Their easy friendship wasn't going to be so simple anymore, and she felt that added weight in her heart, too, but it was bound to happen sometime. Two healthy, single adults couldn't spend that much time together and not start feeling something, could they? That was the explanation for these conflicting emotions inside of her.

She bent down to run a hand across the completed bench and took a moment to look it over and show some enthusiasm.

"I've been thinking, though," Haddie said, straightening. "Paul was very kind to buy you that gift earlier today, and I said no because I wanted you to learn a lesson about behaving well."

"Not in front of Paul!" Timothy pleaded.

"Okay, okay…" Haddie shot Paul a wry smile. "But I was just going to say that you've worked very hard to make this right, and since Paul was kind enough to buy you that tool belt, I thought it might be right for you to have it, after all."

"Really, *Mamm*?" Timothy's eyes lit up.

"*Yah*. Go get it. It's on the counter by the scale."

Timothy dashed over, and Paul stepped closer to her.

"I'm sorry to have messed that up," he said quietly.

"It's okay," she said. "I was being a little bit proud, too. Those boots were more expensive than I'd thought, and I don't have the extra right now."

Paul's strong hand caught her arm and gave her a gentle squeeze. "I can help—"

"I'm fine," she said firmly, then smiled faintly. "But thank you, Paul. I appreciate it. It's under control, though. We have no debt, and the sales are strong. We'll be okay."

"I was told by my sister-in-law that I was to pick up some extra butter today," Paul said.

"You were not," she countered.

"I…was." She could hear the lie in his voice, and his face colored. "Okay, I wasn't. But she'd be very happy if I came home with extra butter, especially the honey almond. Everyone loves it, and it disappears as soon as I bring it back to the house."

"It's my gift," she said.

"I wouldn't hear of it," he said firmly. "I'm paying. And that's final."

He was kind, so kind that it brought a lump to her throat. "I have two pounds left."

"I'll take all of it, and four pounds of plain unsalted, please. I'll bring some to Cecily and Abigail, too."

"All right, then." Haddie went to the fridge to pull it out, and she smiled at her son, who was joyfully tightening the tool belt around his waist.

"I can pull out the hammer, and the screwdriver…" Timothy was talking away to anyone and no one at all as he practiced reaching for tools.

She pulled out a plastic bag and put the butter inside. Then she rang up the total. When he'd paid and she gave him his change, she let her fingers rest in his palm a little longer than she needed to.

"Thank you for all of this, Paul," she said quietly. "I'm sorry I got mad at you like that."

"It's okay."

"I put a few extra little samples of some new butter blends I'm trying in the bag," she added.

"One of them is an orange blend. If they like them, let me know. It will help me decide what to make in bigger batches."

"I'll do that." Paul smiled and took the bag from her hand. "I'm sure I'll see you both at Sunday service."

"*Yah*, of course," she said with a smile.

Paul headed for the door, and he waved once more before he disappeared outside, and Haddie locked the front door after him. When she turned back toward Timothy, he had a smile on his face.

"Do you like it?" she asked him.

"*Yah.* Ask to borrow my wrench. Go ahead, ask me."

"Can I borrow your wrench?" she asked with a low laugh, and her son pulled it out of his belt.

"But give it back right away, because I don't lend tools," Timothy said with a grin, and Haddie couldn't help but laugh and shake her head.

She might not like how close Paul was getting, or the feelings that he was sparking inside of her, but Timothy did look happier.

Paul was helping him in a way that Haddie couldn't, and while she couldn't explain exactly how that made her feel, she was grateful. None of this was Timothy's fault, and seeing him smile like that made her realize that she'd have to figure this out sooner or later.

Maybe Paul and Timothy could be friends, and she could take a step back.

She'd have to pray about it.

Chapter Ten

Sunday dawned crisp and cold. Frost laced the edges of the windows in Haddie's little house, and she had to hurry Timothy along in his morning chores so that they wouldn't be late. But he was tired, as he always was on the weekends, so Haddie accepted the fact that they'd likely arrive late, and cooked up some thick oatmeal and boiled eggs for their breakfast.

Haddie's blue Sunday dress was the same one she'd been married in, and she'd mended it and let it out, and did her best to keep it presentable, but it was past time for a new Sunday dress. She couldn't quite let it go, though. Not yet.

Haddie handed a washcloth to her son and had him wipe his face and neck and behind his ears. He'd had a bath the night before, of course, but she liked him to be extra clean for service.

"Your suspender is twisted," she said. Timothy fixed it. "Better. You look very nice, son. Get your coat. It's time to go."

Services were being held at the Troyer organic, free-range chicken-and-egg farm this week. The service took place in a big, empty barn with three woodstoves to warm the interior, and beyond was the big chicken barn, and contented clucks could be heard all the way into the service. There was something peaceful about it—the sound of nesting poultry filling in the gaps as they bowed for silent prayer.

Haddie usually enjoyed when her friend Ellen Troyer's farm was the host location for their worship services, but this time, she felt a little shy around Ellen. She hadn't quite fixed things with her son, and Paul was a bigger part of her efforts there than she liked to admit to someone like Ellen, who'd gladly see a romance bloom. And if truth be told, Haddie didn't like to admit that she hadn't been able to get through to Timothy on her own.

The first stretch of preaching was done. There would be another sermon later that afternoon by a traveling preacher who was known to be very interesting to listen to. But between services, there would be food, which meant that the women were busy in the kitchen, getting food ready for the whole community.

They tended to keep things simple—soup, sandwiches, donuts and pastries, and hand pies. If lunch was too complicated, the women would never hear a sermon, but if they kept things simple enough, everyone could be fed both physically and spiritually.

Haddie stood in the kitchen at the far end of the large table, assembling sandwiches and putting them into large plastic containers, each layer separated by wax paper. She worked quickly—egg-salad sandwiches on freshly baked white bread, sliced diagonally. The door opened, and a baby's whimper drew Haddie's attention. The women silenced.

It was Abigail dressed in an awkwardly fitting Amish dress. Her grandmother must have only managed to convince her to wear it at the last minute, as Haddie was sure that Cecily would have sewn her a dress herself to make sure she looked the part.

Taylor was in her young mother's arms, squirming against the confines of a thick blanket.

"Hi…" Abigail's gaze sought out Haddie immediately.

"Abigail!" Haddie crossed the room and put her arms around her in a quick hug. "It's so nice you came. Is your grandmother here?"

"She's talking to my dad outside," Abigail said. "But it's cold. These dresses don't do much for that, do they?"

"You get used to it," Haddie said. "Everyone, this is Abigail Ebersole, and her little one is named Taylor."

"*Mammi* said I should come in here and help out," Abigail said, and she looked helplessly down at her baby.

"If it's okay with you, I bet I could find a girl who'd love to hold Taylor for a little while," Haddie replied.

"I'd volunteer." Rose Lapp was thirteen, and she loved holding babies. "I've held your daughter before, actually."

"You have?" Abigail's face colored.

"I did, when she was…visiting my neighbor." But Rose wouldn't be daunted. "She's very sweet. I just adore her. I'd love to hold her a little bit, if you're okay with it."

Abigail hesitated, then nodded. "Okay."

"Hi, you!" Rose said as she eased Taylor

out of Abigail's arms. "You're just as cute as a calf, aren't you? Hi! Yes! Hi!"

Taylor looked up at Rose in mild surprise, but her fussing stopped. Abigail smiled and seemed to relax as Rose abandoned her duties at the counter in favor of cuddling the baby.

"She's a nice girl," Haddie said quietly. "I wouldn't worry. She's got nieces and nephews galore, and she'll have twelve of her own, one day, I'm sure. Let me take your coat."

Abigail allowed Haddie to hang her coat up on top of another coat in the already over-flowing mudroom. The women in the kitchen turned back to their work, and Haddie nodded to the sink.

"Wash your hands, and you can help me with the sandwiches."

Abigail allowed herself to be gently guided through the process, and came to the edge of the kitchen table, where Haddie had been working.

"Now, I'll make sandwiches, and you stack them in the container, okay?"

"Simple enough," Abigail replied, and for a couple of minutes the work went much faster with two more hands at the job. The women fell back into the rhythm of the work. A few said a brief hello to Abigail, but then they went back to their groups, chatting among themselves, and Haddie and Abigail were left in relative privacy in their spot by the table.

Abigail worked silently.

"How are you doing?" Haddie asked quietly.

"I'm okay." The girl's eyes flickered toward Rose, who was pointing at things out the window for Taylor's benefit.

"You sure?" Haddie asked. "I'm a friend, if you need to talk. I remember when my son was tiny—it wasn't easy. No one tells you that part, do they?"

"No, they don't," Abigail agreed. "But it's not just that. I miss my mom a lot."

"Oh…" Haddie reached over and gave Abigail's hand a squeeze. "You would. I'm sorry, sweetie. It must be really hard."

"The hardest thing is that when I ask about my mother's childhood, or what she was like when she was my age, there are no pictures, or anything."

"There wouldn't be," Haddie agreed. "We don't have photos here."

"How do you remember people, then?" Abigail asked helplessly. "Because I find myself forgetting her face, sometimes. And I don't know how that's even possible. I do have some pictures of her of my own, but… I don't know how you all do it."

"We tell stories about them," Haddie replied softly. "We talk about them. We all remember together."

"Even when they're shunned?" The girl turned sad eyes onto Haddie, and Haddie nodded firmly.

"*Yah*, Abigail. Even then. We still love people."

"What was my mother like when she was young?" Abigail asked.

Haddie smiled faintly. "I have to be honest with you, Abigail. Your mother and I were in competition."

"What?" Abigail's eyebrows went up.

"We were the same age," Haddie said. "And she was prettier than I was…" Haddie nudged Abigail's arm fondly. "I don't mind admitting that. She was just beautiful. She had blond hair and blue eyes that shone like moonlight on water. And we were both hoping to marry the same boy."

"Your husband?" Abigail asked. The question was innocent enough.

"Your father," Haddie replied. "Your *daet* was courting me at the time, taking me home from youth events and taking me driving in his buggy. That's how we date here, by the way. So if a boy asked you to go for a drive, you know what that means."

Abigail smiled faintly. "I'm a mother. I doubt that will happen."

Haddie let it drop. Who knew? The heart wanted what it wanted, and Paul was evidence of that.

"Anyway," Haddie went on. "I wasn't a very good match for your father."

"No?" Abigail shot her a sidelong look.

"I had a very strong personality," Haddie said. "I still do. I like things to go my way. I don't like to bend. I have a tendency to think I'm right all the time…"

"You sound like my mom," Abigail said with a sad smile.

"Yah…" That was the problem, wasn't it? Paul's tumultuous marriage with Leah had been the exact thing that Haddie's father had wanted to spare her from.

"Tell me about her," Haddie said softly. "You can talk about your *mamm* with me."

"My mom was tough," Abigail said. "Her boss at the grocery store told her to do this display with a bunch of cans, and my mom said it wouldn't fit in the space, and the boss wouldn't listen to her and yelled at her and told her to just do it. So my mom went to the boss's boss and proved that the request was ridiculous, and then she demanded a written apology for having been yelled at in front of her coworkers and the customers."

"Wow." Haddie shot Abigail a wide-eyed look.

"That was after her boss had been rude to her for like three months because my mom wouldn't respond to his flirting," Abigail said. "He was mad that she wouldn't flirt with him like the other women there did. He used to yell at her all the time after that."

It sounded like a terrible experience all-round. Haddie was her own boss and wouldn't have to deal with anything like that, but she had to wonder what she would do if her situation was different. She was a single mother, too, after all. Leah had been backed into a corner, and Haddie had a personality that snapped back when she was in closed spaces, too, although the Amish way was a less aggressive one.

"We don't tend to deal with things quite that way," Haddie said, "but I can understand why she'd feel like she needed to stand up for herself."

"Other workers got their hours cut if they ever crossed the boss," Abigail said. "And Mom couldn't afford that. We had rent to pay. There were a few times our power got shut off."

Abigail looked around the kitchen. "Not that it would matter here, but it sure mattered to us."

"I understand," Haddie said. She reached for the wax paper and put it down on top of a newly finished layer. "Your mother was taking care of you just as fiercely as she had to. A mother's instinct is strong."

Abigail's face flushed and she didn't answer.

"It does develop over time," Haddie whispered.

"You sure?"

"Positive. We learn as we go," Haddie said. "I'm still learning. My son is ten, and I feel like I'm jogging behind him to keep up."

"That's how I feel with Taylor," Abigail said.

"Then I fully understand." Haddie shot her a smile. "You're a mother, Abigail. Welcome to the group."

Abigail laughed softly. "I'm not sure the others want to welcome me."

"They do," Haddie replied. "Amish women are shy. You'll find that out. They take some time to get to know you, but not because they don't like you. They're just not used to new people."

"You aren't shy."

"I'm not typical, either," Haddie said with a wink.

And neither had Leah been typical, but upon hearing the stories of her battling for respect in her workplace, Haddie's respect for her old rival had grown. She'd been a mother who needed to provide for her daughter, and while others might have taken the easy road and flirted with the boss, Leah wouldn't do it.

She'd made mistakes, but that was a line she wouldn't cross. And she'd been tough enough to fight for her self-respect when there was no one else to stand up for her.

Mothers did what they had to do.

The door opened again, and this time Cecily came inside.

"Let me wash my hands and come help you all!" Cecily called. "What a lovely sermon this morning!"

Haddie exchanged a small smile with Abigail. Most women only realized how strong they really were when they found themselves in a corner. She hoped Abigail had the strength of her departed mother, because while it might be difficult for many men to handle, it was absolutely necessary when a woman needed to provide for her child.

Some women didn't have the luxury of

being meek. And others, like Haddie, couldn't fake it even if they tried.

A half hour later, Paul watched as the women brought out the food—large bowls of pasta salad, bins of sandwiches, bowls of cut fruit and platters of donuts and pastries. His stomach rumbled. The first two sermons of the morning had both gone a little longer than usual, and Paul was hungry. He spotted Cecily arranging a basket of napkins, and Abigail had Taylor in her arms. The baby was looking around happily, seeming to enjoy the chilly air. A couple of younger women were talking to his daughter, and Abigail's face had lit up with a kind of smile he hadn't seen before. Was that what she was like with her friends when she was relaxed? Because if so, she looked just lovely—happy, bright, cheerful. She was getting more comfortable in Redemption, it seemed, and he was glad to see it.

Paul's nieces and a couple of the older boys were playing the game of Snake with some younger children, leading them in a twisting line as they all held hands.

"Hold on!" they called. "Don't let go!"

The children squealed with laughter as the chain broke and the little ones fell into the snow at Abigail's feet, and she laughed, stepping aside to keep from trampling the tumbling *kinner*.

"She's having fun."

He looked over as Haddie stepped up beside him. She held up a napkin with a large donut on it.

"For me?" he said.

She gave a nod, and he took the donut gratefully. "*Yah*, she looks like she's settling in, doesn't she?"

"I talked to her a little while in the kitchen," Haddie said. "I think she'll be just fine. She's got—" Haddie pressed her lips together "—she's got the gumption that she's going to need."

"How is Timothy?" Paul asked.

"Very happy with his new tools," she said.

He hesitated. "Again, I'm sorry about that."

Haddie shook her head. "It's fine. Maybe he needed more encouragement than discipline this time around. He's made the bench, and we'll bring it to the school when I drop him off on Monday. Maybe all this trouble is over now."

"Maybe," Paul said with a nod.

"Why do you say it like that?" she asked.

Paul shrugged. "I was just agreeing with you. Why?"

Haddie sighed. "Maybe I want more reassurance that everything will be smooth from here on out, but I don't think that's very realistic, do you?"

"Probably not." He cast her a smile. "But he's a good boy. That's part of growing up—learning things the hard way now when the stakes are lower. It's better than learning it later on when there can be real damage to his future."

"That's a good point," she said.

Paul's gaze moved over to his daughter, and then past her. Paul spotted a local man named Abe Hines striding across the snow-flattened grass, pulling a boy along on either side. Paul recognized both *kinner* right away—it was Simon and Timothy. The boys were marching along resignedly enough, and Paul guessed that they didn't have much choice.

"Uh-oh," Paul said.

Haddie followed his gaze, and she suddenly stilled. Paul looked over at her, and her face was pale, but her eyes were flashing fire. Haddie didn't wait for them to get to her—she marched over to Abe Hines and caught her son's other arm, taking custody of him. Abe brought Simon over to Paul.

"I don't see your brother around," Abe said. "So I'll hand him over to you."

Simon's nose was bloody, and he had a

scrape across one hand. His hair was ruffled, and his felt hat was gone. A smear of blood on the front of his white shirt visible under his undone jacket would be a whole other conversation with his mother when she got to his laundry.

"What happened?" Paul asked.

"Simon and Timothy Petersheim were having a fistfight out there behind the barn," Abe said. "I had to pull them apart."

"A fight?" Paul looked down at Simon, eyebrows raised, then he glanced to Abe. "Thanks for bringing him over. I'll take care of it."

He glanced at Haddie, and they exchanged a look before she pulled Timothy aside to talk to him more privately. Abe gave Paul a nod and headed back the way he'd come.

Paul crossed his arms and looked down at Simon.

"So?" he said. "Explain yourself."

"Timothy's a pest!" Simon said. "He won't quit nagging at me, and slapping my hat, and tripping me."

"So you decided to fight him?" Paul said. "Since when is being annoying reason for a fight like that?"

"He fought *me*!" Simon said earnestly. "He's trouble! He's always doing something bad! I'm not the problem! He is! He's so jealous that *Daet* does stuff with me that he can't stand it!"

This didn't quite jibe with the young man Paul had been helping to build a bench. Timothy wasn't a mean boy…

"So why is he hearing about all the stuff your *daet* does with you?" Paul asked.

"I can't mention my own *daet*?" Simon asked. "Really? I can't even mention something that involves my father because Timothy is too sensitive about it? That's not fair. I wasn't even talking to him!"

Paul sighed. "He's been through a lot."

"*Yah!* Two years ago!" Simon snapped. "I'm sorry he lost his *daet*. I am. But that's not an excuse to be a pain to everyone for the rest of his life, is it?"

Paul rubbed a hand over his beard, thinking.

"So he started it?" Paul asked.

"*Yah!* He's been pestering me for months! And he slapped my hat off, and I hit him. So I'm sorry I did that, but I'd had enough." Simon scowled over his shoulder in Timothy's direction.

Timothy had been in trouble at school, acting out and being generally difficult.

"So what was I supposed to do?" Simon demanded.

"Tell an adult," Paul replied.

"What adult? No one was around!" Simon shook his head. "Sometimes you just have to take care of something yourself. And that's what I did. So you can tell my *daet* whatever you want to tell him, I'm telling him the truth. And he's not going to be mad at me for this."

Paul sighed. "Well, you've got a bloody nose, so I suggest you go get cleaned up. You can take this up with your father. He'll sort you out, I'm sure."

And Simon was right—Josh wasn't going to punish his son for standing up for himself when another boy was pushing him around. It certainly did sound like Timothy was the problem.

Simon headed off toward the house, and Paul looked up to see Timothy marching off toward the buggies. Haddie stood with her arms crossed over her chest, but her face had lost the earlier anger. She looked ready to cry, and his heart tugged toward her.

"Are you leaving?" Paul asked as he walked up to where she stood.

"*Yah*, we're going home." Her voice was tight. "That Simon had better leave my son alone, though, Paul. Enough is enough. Timothy has enough he's dealing with without being bullied."

Well, that was a different version of events.

"From what I hear, Timothy has been picking on Simon," Paul said, keeping his voice low.

Haddie shot him an incredulous look. "What? My son just told me that the boy who's been picking on him at school all this time was your nephew. He said that he kept teasing him and telling him that I need to get married again so that he'll have another *daet*. If that isn't inappropriate, I don't know what is!"

"Simon?" Paul looked in the direction of where his nephew had disappeared into the house. "Timothy said that?"

"*Yah*, Timothy told me everything," she said. "And he'd had enough. So he finally stood up for himself."

"That's not the story that I heard," Paul said. "Can I talk to Timothy and see what he says?"

Something changed in Haddie's expression, and she met his gaze, but the anger was back. "No. I don't think so."

"One of them is lying," Paul said. "I'm just trying to figure out what's going on."

"So it's Timothy who's lying?" Haddie's eyebrows went up. "That's the assumption? Timothy isn't a bad boy. He's been having a tough time at school, and he's sensitive. He's not some hulking bully looking for some smaller boy to pick on. That isn't what he's like! He told me the truth, and I believe him."

"They're boys!" Paul said. "Sometimes they lie!"

"Then have a discussion about honesty with Simon," she snapped. "My son is not lying to me."

"Your son left Simon with a bloody nose!" Paul retorted.

"Simon left Timothy with a black eye!" she countered. "Paul, this is my personal business to handle with my son as I see fit. Thank you for all you've done, but you need to leave this to me. If Josh or Lorena want to talk to me about this, parent to parent, they know where to find me."

Paul felt the words like a slap. "Really?"

"You might have spent some time with my son," Haddie said, her voice shaking, "and you might think he's a great boy when you're doing something you enjoy with him like woodworking, but that doesn't make you any kind of expert on how my son thinks or feels. I'm the one who's raising him. I'm the one who tucks him into bed at night, and talks to him about right and wrong. I'm the one who'd lie down and die for him. So don't think you know better about my child just because you had the pleasure of getting to know him a little bit!"

"Haddie, I think Timothy is a great kid—"

Haddie gave him a warning look, then turned and swept off in the direction of the buggies. He watched her go, his heart sinking. Had he handled that so badly? He couldn't declare Simon some kind of little villain just to make another boy happy, either. There were two sides to this story, and maybe Paul was the only one emotionally removed enough to see that.

He looked down at the untouched donut still in his hand. He'd forgotten he even had it, and he took a bite. Her walls had gone up, and he felt that old helplessness he used to feel when he was fighting with Leah.

Just because a woman had strong opinions didn't make her always right. It just made it harder to find some common ground, and maybe he should see this as a good reminder. He always was drawn to a certain type of woman, but eighteen years didn't change the outcome. He might be mild-mannered, but he wasn't willing to just knuckle under, either.

"What happened?"

He turned to see Cecily looking in the same direction he was.

"The boys had a fistfight," he replied.

"*Yah*, I saw them both—looks like it was

evenly matched. Their parents will sort them out, I'm sure."

Paul pressed his lips together. And he wasn't either of these boys' father. Why did the reminder sting so much? He had a daughter of his own—he should be focusing on her.

"A word to the wise?" Cecily said.

"Sure."

"Don't let the squabbles of *kinner* turn into squabbles between adults," Cecily said. "The *kinner* will have made up long before the adults ever do. It's a waste of arguing, is what it is." Cecily gave him a pointed look, then angled her head toward the food. "Better come eat before the food is gone."

Paul didn't feel like eating anymore—his stomach was tied up with knots of irritation. He should just let Haddie deal with things on her own. Why did it suddenly matter to him how she parented her son?

But it did because he cared about Haddie in a way that filled him up and spilled over, and he cared about Timothy, too. Timothy and Simon obviously had some issues to work out, but that didn't mean that Paul thought less of Timothy. He was a great kid, but no ten-year-old boy was perfect.

Least of all Simon.

He sighed.

Haddie was Timothy's mother, and Paul was just the man who was trying to fix a mistake he'd made with a kitten in her shop. This wasn't his business…even if he wished he could help. It might be time to take a step back and remember his position.

He wasn't the *daet* here. He wasn't Haddie's man, either. As much as his heart might want to argue otherwise, this wasn't his business.

Chapter Eleven

The next morning, Paul flicked the reins, hurrying his horses along on the way into town. The air was cold, but the sun shone warm and golden off the frosted trees and fence posts, promising a warmer day ahead. Simon was at his side this morning, silent. Normally Simon talked quite a lot, especially if he got to come along with his uncle somewhere, but this morning was more somber. This wasn't coming along for the fun of it, missing school in order to experience some aspect of running the farm with his uncle. This was about making things right from yesterday.

There was one last container of cream reserved for Petersheim Creamery, as always. Paul had finished all the other deliveries, and he'd arranged his route so that Haddie's shop was the last one for the last month or two.

He'd been enjoying her company—stopping in for a cup of coffee sometimes…or just hoping she'd offer. Their friendship had been slowly growing, and he'd only thought of it as that—a friendship—until Barnabas had chased Thimble, and then he'd started to notice things about Haddie that he hadn't before, like the softness underneath that competent, decisive exterior.

Paul tried to push back his uncomfortable feelings. He'd felt the change between him and Haddie—something invisible but absolutely sure, and he knew what it felt like when a wall went up between a man and a woman. His entire first year of marriage before Leah left had been lived like there had been a barn wall between them.

He shouldn't feel this as keenly as he did, but he missed what had been growing. Friendship, and lately something more… This wasn't about his past mistakes, or even his first wife. This was about something fresh and new that had been budding between him and Haddie, and he wasn't ready to let it go.

"How come you aren't working on the farm as much?" Simon asked, breaking him out of his thoughts.

"I'm helping Haddie Petersheim fix up her shop after Thimble ruined it."

"Thimble…" Simon muttered.

"Don't you put your nose up about that," Paul said. "Very small things can cause a whole lot of damage in life. You remember that."

"Yah." Simon sighed.

"You're doing the right thing, Simon," Paul said. "I'm proud of you for doing this."

Simon didn't answer, and Paul didn't really expect him to. This wasn't going to be easy for Simon, but Josh had insisted that his son make this right. Paul had nothing to do with it. This morning, Josh had asked that Paul take Simon with him so that Simon could apologize to Haddie. That was all.

"One thing you need to remember," Paul said as he reined in his horse in at a four-way stop. He waited until two cars had passed in front of him, then flicked his reins and they started forward again. "Haddie Petersheim lost her husband. So she's been on her own. She's doing her best, but she's not like your *mamm*, who has your *daet*, and your brothers, and me—all of us—working hard to keep things running. Haddie has to do it all by herself. That's a lot for one woman to take care of. That means that Timothy has to do a whole lot more than you do to help his *mamm*. And maybe he worries more, too."

"I know," Simon said. "*Mamm* talked to me about that."

"She did?"

Simon nodded. "She said that *Gott* wants us men to take care of our women, but there are some women who have to take care of themselves, and that *Gott* commands us to keep them in mind, too. And if I'm going to be an upstanding man in this community, then I'd better start thinking a bit differently."

It sounded like he'd gotten quite a good lecture last night. Paul was impressed. A light was burning in the storefront of Petersheim Creamery, but Paul couldn't see Haddie. She'd be in the back of the shop getting ready to start churning. He knew her routine well enough by now, and he noticed that his own heartbeat had sped up as he steered the horse into the lane that led behind the creamery, and reined him in.

Paul hopped down, tied the horse to a hitching post and then climbed into the back of the wagon to hoist down the can of cream. Simon waited until Paul was back on the ground again, and Paul nodded to the door.

"Knock," he said.

"Me?" Simon's eyes had lost the attitude from earlier, and he now looked up at the building with trepidation.

"My hands are full. Go on."

Simon headed up the steps and knocked twice. The door opened and Haddie looked down at Simon in surprise.

"Simon?" Haddie stepped back. "Come on in."

She looked up at Paul and gave him a hesitant smile.

"Good morning," Paul said. "I have your cream."

"Thank you."

Was it that Simon was with him, or was it their argument from yesterday? But he felt the tension in the air still, and he wanted to clear it, if he could.

Paul followed his nephew into the shop, and he put the heavy tin of cream down on the table where he always left it. Haddie had her bowl of utensils already steaming on the counter, and her gaze flickered up toward Paul questioningly.

"Simon wanted to say something to you," Paul said. "Go on, Simon."

"I'm—" Simon's voice cracked. "I'm very sorry for fighting with your son. It was wrong of me. I should have been more patient like a Christian instead of fighting with him."

"Thank you for that," Haddie said, but her expression hadn't softened.

Simon swallowed. "I blamed it on him. And it wasn't really all his fault. We've been fighting a lot. Not like…hitting. But I mean, we've been not getting along really well. And part of it is because Timothy bugs me and part of it is because I've been bugging him right back. So it's not all his fault. When we got into that fight yesterday, he'd told me about his new tools, and I got… I got mad. I don't know why."

"A little jealous, maybe?" Paul asked quietly.

"Maybe." Simon's cheeks grew red. "*Yah*, I was jealous. And I said something awful, and that's why he hit me first."

"What did you say?" Haddie asked softly.

Tears welled in Simon's eyes. "I said my uncle Paul wasn't his *daet*, so he should stop pretending he had one." His chin trembled. "It was really mean, and I'm really sorry I said it."

Tears welled in Haddie's eyes, too, and she bent down to Simon's level.

"That wasn't easy for you to tell me, was it?"

The boy shook his head.

"I'm proud of you for telling me the whole truth, Simon," she said. "You chose the right thing, and I think you're a good boy. That's what I think. Okay?"

Simon nodded.

"And I forgive you," she added, and she put her arms around him and gave him a squeeze. Tears leaked down Simon's cheeks, and Paul felt a lump in his own throat.

"That isn't all, though," Simon said, his voice shaking. "My *mamm* says I have to tell you the rest, even though I said it was tattling."

Haddie's gaze flickered toward Paul again.

"I know where he goes at lunch," Simon whispered.

Paul startled at that revelation, and he exchanged a surprised look with Haddie.

"You know?" Paul said.

"*Yah*, I followed him once," Simon said. "I just wanted to see where he went. And it's to the graveyard."

Paul's heart sank. The graveyard… There was only one for their community, so there was no question about which graveyard the boy was talking about. It was a place every good member of their community expected to rest one day. Leah hadn't been buried there because she was shunned, but her mother had spread her ashes just outside the fence—it was as close to bringing her home as Cecily had been able to manage. That graveyard was where Timothy's father was buried, too.

"That's a long walk from the school," Paul

murmured. It was all he could think to say, because the thought of Timothy trudging out there alone made his throat thick with emotion.

"It's where he goes," Simon said defensively. "I never told anyone. I'm not that bad. But I'm not lying. *Mamm* said it was important that I tell Timothy's mother. I wouldn't lie."

"I know, I know." He put a steadying hand on Timothy's shoulder.

There was a certain loyalty between boys, even when they were rivals. Paul remembered those old boyish honor codes, and Simon was right—tattling was about the worst thing a boy could do, no matter whom he was tattling on, and Simon was breaking that code today because his *mamm* had told him he needed to.

"He goes to the graveyard…" Haddie looked up at Paul, all those earlier walls crumbling, and it was like he could see her heart cracking in two along with them. "I haven't gone back since I buried Job. He goes there alone?"

Paul swallowed. There was nothing he could say, but then Haddie seemed to rally.

She looked toward Simon. "It's okay, Simon. Thank you for telling me. I needed to know."

"Could you take that empty tin back out to the wagon, Simon?" Paul asked.

"*Yah*. Okay." Simon picked up the waiting

empty tin and headed back outside. For a moment, Paul and Haddie were silent.

"I'm sorry about yesterday," Paul said. "I didn't mean to sound the way I did. Timothy is going through a lot, and obviously Simon was being a lot meaner to him than I realized. I feel terrible."

"Simon isn't a bad boy," Haddie said quietly. "He's learning, too."

Paul nodded, and he cast Haddie a hopeful smile. "Are we friends still?"

"Yah." She smiled and nodded. "Of course, Paul."

But friendship was very likely where this needed to stay. Maybe their argument was a good thing, because it could allow them to reset their relationship back where it needed to be, no matter how attracted to her he was.

"I'll come by later on today and finish the last of the shelving," he said. "It'll be completely done by tonight. That's a promise."

"Oh…will it?" There was something in her voice that he couldn't quite identify. Was she feeling sad to have their time together end, too?

"Yah," he said. "I hope you'll be happy with the finished product. I've done my best."

"It's looking very nice." She licked her lips. He looked down at her, and all he was ever able to think about these days was his own longing to kiss her all over again.

He had to stop this.

"I'll see you later on," he said, and he took a purposeful step toward the door.

"Thank you, Paul."

Paul joined his nephew in the wagon, and with one last look toward the window, where he could see Haddie looking out at them, he flicked the reins.

"Time to get you to school," Paul said.

"Yah."

"Do you feel better now?" Paul asked.

"I think I do," Simon said. "At least I know I tried to make it right. I won't be picking on Timothy anymore, even if he picks on me."

"I'm glad to hear it."

Maybe they'd resolved this problem between the boys, at least, even if whatever was stewing between them as adults didn't seem quite so easy to navigate.

As they pulled onto a quiet Main Street, Paul settled back into his seat and looked out at a group of *Englisher* teenagers who were eating some fast food out of a bag on some benches. Funny—he'd never looked at *Englisher* teenagers as if they had anything to do with his life in the past. He used to look right past them, but these days he looked a little bit closer.

There were three boys and two girls, and as he leaned forward to look at them, he startled. One of the girls, who was dressed in blue jeans and a puffy pink coat, was eating a breakfast sandwich, and when she raised her gaze, she startled, too.

"Abigail?" He reined in his horse and pulled to the side of the street. The horse stamped impatiently.

"Dad? What are you doing here?" Abigail asked, and she moved away from the group. The teens stared at him, wide-eyed.

"Is that my cousin?" Simon asked from beside him.

"*Yah*, this is your cousin. Come say hello."

Abigail crossed the street, and Paul hopped down from the wagon.

"What are you doing out here?" he asked.

"My friends stopped by the house to take me out for breakfast," she said.

"Is your *mammi* babysitting Taylor this morning?"

She nodded. "I miss seeing friends."

"I'm glad you could see them," he replied. "This is your cousin Simon. He's my brother Josh's youngest son. I don't think you saw him on Sunday."

Simon and Abigail exchanged some shy hellos, and Paul dug inside his coat and pulled out her cell phone. He handed it over.

"I was going to bring this to you today," he said. "It's all charged up."

Simon looked warily toward the cell phone. "She has a cell phone?"

"Simon, she isn't Amish," Paul replied, and he shot his daughter a reassuring smile. "I won't keep you from your friends. But I'm glad to see you. Maybe you'd like to come visit with your other cousins one of these days. Everyone is excited to get to know you better."

"I'm not going to be what they expect..." Abigail said. "I don't normally dress in Amish clothes like I did on Sunday."

"Actually, you're exactly what we expected," Simon said brazenly. "Uncle Paul said you were as *English* as *English* could be. And that's you."

Abigail laughed and wagged a finger at Simon. "I like you."

Simon blushed in response, and Abigail looked back toward her friends. They were all staring, and Paul knew it was time to let her get back to her plans. She was old enough to be on a *Rumspringa*, if she'd been Amish. She could eat some fast food with friends if she wanted to.

"Well… I'll see you later on," Paul said, and he climbed back up into the wagon again. "I'll come by and visit."

"Thanks, Dad."

Paul watched as Abigail crossed the street, and he noticed the sour looks the other teenagers cast in his direction. They didn't like him—that was clear. Was it because he was the absentee father, or was there something more to it?

Abigail looked over her shoulder at him once more, then turned back to her friends as their wagon rattled on past.

"Is she going to be Amish?" Simon asked.

But Paul wasn't sure that he could make up for all those years he was absent from her life as easily as that. He looked over his shoulder, and the teens disappeared from sight.

"You know, Simon," Paul said, "I'm not going to lie to you. She might never be Amish. She wants to finish high school and go to college… I don't think she wants to be an Amish wife. But no matter what happens, she's going to be a member of this family. She belongs to us."

"Even if she isn't Amish?" Simon asked.

"Even if she isn't Amish."

Abigail was his daughter—no matter what. She'd been raised *English*—it wasn't the same as if he'd raised her here, and the community wouldn't expect her to follow their ways. Paul needed to take care of the family *Gott* had given him. That was what he should do.

So why did his heart keep trying to expand and pull in Haddie and Timothy, too?

Haddie left the store with a sign in the window saying that she'd be back in an hour and a half. This was the busy time of day, the noon hour, when people had their breaks from work and came to run their errands. But this was also the time that Timothy slipped off the school playground, and she wouldn't lose this chance.

"Haddie, are you closing up?" Ellen Troyer asked. The slim woman stood at the side of the building, a cloth shopping bag in one hand, and her thick shawl pulled close around her with the other. She watched as Haddie tightened the last strap on her horse's tack. "I just needed to buy some butter."

"I'm in a hurry, Ellen," Haddie said. "I'm sorry! I'll be back in a couple of hours."

Ellen didn't pursue it, but her expression was one of surprise as Haddie hoisted herself up in the seat and flicked the reins.

"I'm sorry!" Haddie repeated as the horse clopped toward her friend.

"Is there a problem?" Ellen asked, squinting in the sunlight. "Is there anything I can do?"

"I'll be back!" Haddie replied. "Everything is okay!"

This was private—she wouldn't explain herself to anyone. If she went back to sell Ellen some butter, someone else would come in and then someone else, and she'd never be able to get away. She saw an *Englisher* couple stop and read her sign in the window, then check their watches. Haddie turned her horse in the direction of Redemption's town limits.

The graveyard was a mile outside of town, and two miles from the school. It was located in a field of wildgrass, cradled by a copse of trees on the east, and separated by a whitewashed wooden fence from the expanse of farmland rolling out to the west. Amish burials were simple affairs. The gravestones gave names and dates, nothing more. There were no stories told on their gravestones—those were told by the people who had known the deceased, or by the family members who told stories about grandparents, great-grandparents, great-aunts and uncles... People kept memories alive, not stone.

So Job's gravestone was just like the others, just a little newer. After the ceremony to bury her husband in that hand-dug grave, she'd not come back. For Haddie, Job's memory wasn't out here in the graveyard, it was back there in the shop, in their little house, in the recipes for butter blends, and in that old chipped coffee mug he'd drunk out of every morning.

But maybe it was different for Timothy. She hadn't considered that, but she did now as her horse's hooves clopped down the paved road, and her heart turned toward those sweet memories with the husband she'd loved.

The road that led to the graveyard was empty. Beyond the fence, and farther out into the field, cattle were eating out of a feeder that was topped with a crust of snow still. Life was going on as it always did. At first, Haddie didn't see anyone, and she wondered if maybe Timothy had stopped his little ritual, but then she spotted him. He was crouched down next to his father's gravestone, his back to her. He turned as the horse's hooves hit gravel, and he slowly stood up.

His face was pale, his eyes large, and Haddie reined in the horse and tied off her reins. Timothy's expression was a cautious one—he was afraid he was in trouble, no doubt. And he should be, running away from school property. But how could she reprimand him when she understood his grief?

Haddie jumped down to the ground, pulling her shawl closer around her body to cut out the biting wind.

"Timothy!" she called, and her voice whipped away from her.

Timothy started slowly toward her, his shoulders slumped, and Haddie walked into the graveyard, weaving through the graves until she met him.

"I'm sorry, *Mamm*," Timothy said. "I know you said not to leave school, but—"

He looked over his shoulder, back toward that familiar gravestone, and Haddie's eyes locked on it, too, her heart stopping in her chest. For a moment, they both just looked at it, and then Haddie put an arm around her son's slender shoulders. He leaned his head against her side.

"You miss your *daet*," she said quietly.

Timothy didn't answer, but he exhaled a shuddering breath.

"What do you do when you come here?" she asked.

"I tell *Daet* about things," Timothy said. "I tell him about school, and about fighting with Simon, and about my teacher, and about Paul…"

"Is Simon still bothering you?" she asked. He'd only come to apologize to her that morning, and she'd hoped it would change things at school.

"Not today. Yet."

"What do you think your *daet* would tell you?" she asked.

"To be the bigger man," Timothy whispered. "And to have self-control."

"But Simon's been teasing you about not having a *daet*, hasn't he?"

Timothy looked up at her in surprise. "How did you know?"

"Never mind how," she said. "*Mamms* have their ways. It was mean of him to tease you like that."

Timothy sighed.

"Does it make you feel better to talk to *Daet* here?" she asked.

"Not really." Timothy looked up at her with tears in his eyes. "It just feels like the right place to feel sad."

Haddie squatted down and looked up into her son's blotchy face.

"Timothy, I don't know anyone on this earth who loved you more than your *daet*. Besides me, that is. He thought about you constantly. He bragged about you to all his friends, and his deepest wish for you was that you'd grow up to be a *Gott*-fearing man," she said.

"I know."

"Sometimes, we lose our *daets* earlier than we'd like," Haddie said quietly. "I know you didn't have your *daet* as long as either of us wanted, but *Gott* let you see what a good *daet* looks like, and how he acts, and how he puts his family first. One day, you'll be a *daet* and have *kinner* of your own, and because you had such a good father, you'll know how to do it. That is *Gott*'s gift to you."

"I still feel like I need him, though," Timothy said, his voice trembling.

"I know," she murmured. "You aren't alone, son. You have *me*."

Timothy hitched his shoulders up against an icy blast of wind, and Haddie nudged him toward the buggy.

"Let's get you back to school," she said quietly.

But as she turned, she spotted another small form standing by the entrance to the graveyard, and she recognized him right away.

"What's Simon doing here?" Timothy muttered.

"I don't know," she said. "I guess I'll be taking you both back to school."

Simon clamped a hand down on top of his felt hat, and his ears were red from the cold. Timothy eyed the other boy uncomfortably, and as they approached the buggy, Simon came up to meet them.

"Hi," Simon said.

"Did you follow me?" Timothy demanded.

"Yah." Simon shrugged. "So what?"

"So this is private!" Timothy snapped, and for a moment, they looked like they were ready to fight again, both of their eyes blazing. But then Simon dropped his gaze first, and Timothy looked at the other boy in unveiled surprise.

"I'm sorry I said that stuff on Sunday," Simon said. "I didn't mean it."

"Yah, you did. Or you wouldn't have said it."

"No, I was mad," Simon replied. "And I told your *mamm* that I started it, so—so I am, too, sorry I said it."

"You told her you started it?" Timothy dug a toe into the gravel.

"Yah… My uncle brought me over to tell her the truth."

"Oh."

"So, I'm sorry."

"It's okay." Timothy's shoulders relaxed a little bit. Ten-year-old boys weren't terribly eloquent communicators, and more was being said between the two boys with their body language than with their actual words.

They'd both relaxed in their stances, and they squinted as they eyed each other.

"So, um…" Simon rubbed a gloved hand across his cheek. "You're gonna be late to school again. And the teacher is going to be mad."

"Yup." Timothy straightened his spine. "I'm used to it."

"I figured if we both got back late, then we'd both have to clean the desks after school, and you wouldn't have to do it by yourself this time."

Tears misted Haddie's eyes, and she blinked them back. "I'll drive you both back to school. You won't be quite so late that way."

Timothy kicked a stone and looked toward the road. "If I walked here, I can walk back."

"*Yah*, it's not so far," Simon agreed. "I don't mind washing desks."

"It's not so bad." Timothy shot Simon a grin, and Haddie thought she saw the spark of something close to friendship there between these two little rebels.

"All right," she said. "But you get walking back now! No lollygagging. And no more leaving school property—you hear me?"

"Yes, *Mamm*."

"We won't."

"Okay, then." Haddie nodded toward the road. "You'd better get moving."

The boys started back down the road at a quick pace, side by side. Their heads were angled together as they talked about things they'd never discuss in front of her. Driving them back would spare them some cold and maybe some punishment, but it would also rob them of this opportunity to endure hardship together. That was bonding.

For a couple of minutes she watched as the boys' backs got smaller and smaller as they hurried toward school, their black felt hats bobbing in the cold wind. And then she looked back toward Job's grave.

She wove her way through the graves once more and stopped in front of that stone. Job wasn't here. She knew that. This was just a resting place for bones. But there was something oddly comforting at the thought of being able to say something—anything—to Job again.

"I miss you," she whispered.

The only answer was the far-off lowing of the cattle, and the whistle of the frigid wind.

"Timothy is a good boy," she added, her voice a little stronger now. "You'd be so proud of him, Job. He's got a good heart, and every day he's a little bit taller. He wants to be a good boy, and that's what matters most, isn't it? That's what you always said…"

And the words kept flowing out of her, that pent-up torrent of things she'd wanted to share with her husband, but couldn't anymore. She told him about Timothy, mostly, about his way of seeing things, and the funny things he said. She told him about the kitten named Thimble and old Barnabas chasing her through the shop. She told him about Paul rebuilding the shelves, and his kindness.

"I'm not good at letting other people do things for me," she said. "It was different with you. But now that I'm on my own, I just…" She wiped a tear from her cheek. "It's not the same, Job."

She thought about Paul, about his kiss, about his strength and his way of making her blush…and remembered her father's advice all those years ago. He'd been right, of course.

Could she tell Job about Paul, and the way he made her feel? Could she confess her own weakness, of longing to be loved again?

But Job couldn't give her any guidance, or forgiveness, or even permission—that had to come from *Gott*.

"I'm going to do my best without you," she said, and her voice caught. "Rest in peace, my love."

Then she made her way back toward her buggy. She had a shop to run, and butter to sell, and a life to keep on living, even when it hurt.

Chapter Twelve

Paul ran a rag over the last shelf and stood back to survey his handiwork. This shop looked brand-new. His shelves were sturdy, straight and polished to a shine. He'd built a freestanding shelf with three sides, as well, for added display space, and he was proud of his work. Haddie wouldn't have any trouble with these shelves toppling, and they looked good.

Paul looked down at Barnabas, who was lying by the door. The dog seemed to have accepted Paul as safe, because even when Paul had come inside to find Haddie gone and the store empty except for the old hound, Barnabas had done nothing more than give Paul a sniff and lie back down.

"You won't be able to knock these over," Paul said. He'd secured each shelf to the wall, and with three sides, the freestanding unit was immoveable.

Barnabas suddenly lifted his head, listened and then got to his feet. It was then that Paul heard the sound of a horse's hooves.

"You know that horse, don't you?" Paul said, and he bent down to scratch Barnabas behind the ears. "It sounds like Haddie's back."

A few customers had come to the door while he was working. They'd tapped on the windowpane, and he'd had to tell them that Haddie was gone for a little while, and he couldn't help them. Doubtlessly, there would be quite a few customers who came back again.

Paul headed out the side door to where Haddie had reined in her horse. She was already unbuckling the straps, and he moved to help her.

"You left the side door open, so I hope you don't mind, but I finished everything up," Paul said. "I thought it would be better to get it done earlier than later."

"You did?" She paused, straightened. There was something in her gaze that made his heart stutter, but Paul continued the work and unbuckled the last strap, easing the tracing lines off the horse's back.

"I hope you like it." Paul stroked the horse's coat and gave her rump a pat to send her into her waiting stall. "Where did you go? Is everything okay?"

"I went to the graveyard," she said. "Timothy was there… So was Simon."

"Simon?" Paul frowned. He'd talked to the boy himself about being nicer to Timothy.

"It's okay." She seemed to read the worry in his voice. "They've…bonded. They're getting into trouble together by getting back to school late."

Paul ran that information over in his mind. "Simon's trying to make it up to your son, take some of the punishment. For boys, that's an apology."

"Is it really?" She smiled.

"They're noble at heart," Paul said. "Boys want to be the hero. They want to fix things, suffer for the cause, if they have to. They aren't so different from grown men in that respect."

"Are you really so willing to fling yourself into harm's way?" she asked with a teasing smile.

"For the right cause, I certainly will," Paul said. "For the right woman."

Haddie's cheeks pinked.

Paul didn't know why he was saying all of this. He shouldn't…but his work here was done, and that meant that he wouldn't be seeing her every day anymore beyond dropping off the cream, or perhaps coming to her for some advice. But he couldn't overdo that. Their time together on a daily basis was about to end.

"Well, speaking of suffering for a cause," Haddie said, "the boys will likely be washing desks after school today."

Paul smiled. "As long as they chose it, they'll be friends for life now."

"I'm glad they'll be friends," she said. "Timothy needs that right now."

Paul's mind went back to the boy who'd worked so hard at his side. Timothy wasn't a bad kid, but he was hurting. He hoped that the rest of the community could see the good in him, too, because if a boy was treated like he was bad for too long, he started to be a self-fulfilling prophecy, and Paul wanted better for Timothy than that.

"Is he okay?" Paul asked. "If he was at the graveyard—"

"*Yah*. He is." Haddie sucked in a deep breath, but her eyes didn't look as confident as her words sounded. "I think he is, I mean. He's missing his *daet*, and I can't fix that for him. But that's what it comes down to."

"Is there anything I can do?" he asked.

"It's probably best that you didn't," she said. "I don't want to confuse him...you know?"

Because Timothy wanted a *daet*.

Haddie looked toward the shop, then down at her watch. "I should get back in there."

"Let me show you what I've done," he said, and he led the way back to the stop.

Paul watched Haddie as she walked around her new shop front, running her hand over the smooth shelves. Her face broke into a smile and she looked at Paul with tears in her eyes.

"Paul, this is…" She shook her head. "This is beautiful. I can't thank you enough!"

"It's nothing," he said. It wasn't, though. This had been his very best effort, and he'd prayed the whole time he worked that his humble hands would produce something beautiful for her. "I did something else for you—"

He led the way over to the counter where she served her customers, and he pulled out the scale. He'd had a little plate engraved to put on the bottom of her scale. Haddie picked it up and turned it over. A smile touched her lips.

"'A just weight and balance are the Lord's,'" she said, reading the engraving.

"That verse reminded me of you," he said.

"Fair business practices?" she asked faintly.

Paul chuckled. "No. You're honest in more than your business dealings, Haddie. You're straightforward. You say what you mean. Your yes means yes and your no means no. *Gott* blesses honesty, and I do very sincerely pray that He blesses you."

"Oh, Paul…" She looked up at him, then around at the shop again. "This shop is really becoming mine, isn't it?"

"Of course, it's yours," he replied.

"I mean, before it was Job's, and then it was ours, and I think I was holding on to that feeling—of this being the shop Job and I had together. But it's changed—" She looked around at the new cabinetry. "It really is a new start."

"Is that a good thing?" he asked hesitantly.

"It's…" She looked like she was thinking for a moment, then she nodded. "*Yah*, it's a good thing."

Paul dropped his gaze to meet hers. The sweetness in her eyes made his heart skip a beat.

"I'm glad you like it," he said.

The customers who had promised to come back hadn't returned yet, and Paul looked toward the window, grateful for a few extra minutes without interruption.

"Haddie," he said. "Maybe I could continue helping you…"

Haddie stilled. "How?"

"With Timothy?" he suggested. "I could take him to the dairy, show him how to deal with cattle and farm chores. It's a good thing for a boy to know."

"It is…" Haddie hesitated. Was she considering it?

"I can show him how to make some simple pieces of furniture," he went on. "Every boy should know how to make a rocking chair or a stool. I thought he might like that."

"And if he starts hoping you'll be his new father?" she asked.

"I don't know. We aren't there yet," he replied. He didn't want to think about the more complicated aspects of the plan right now. He just didn't want this to be goodbye.

Haddie licked her lips. "We'd be playing with fire, Paul."

Paul shrugged. "Maybe I don't mind that."

"No, I mean, we'd be in close proximity, and it would be difficult to keep things properly friendly." She looked so serious that he almost laughed. Did she really think he was that naive?

"Haddie, I know what you meant." A slow smile tugged at the corners of his lips. "I'm not some naive kid. I'm older than you."

"Oh." Her face reddened.

"And maybe I want to," he repeated. "I like being around you. I like…making you smile. I like tasting your butter, and hearing what you think about things. I want more of it."

Haddie dropped her gaze. "You're flirting now."

"I'm honest, too," he said, his voice low. "I'm just saying what I feel."

Paul stepped closer and slipped a hand around her waist. Haddie looked up at him, and then her gaze flickered down to his lips. She was thinking what he was, it seemed, and he dipped his head down and caught her lips with his. She let out a little sigh, and he pulled her in closer. He meant this kiss—it wasn't an accident, or fooling around. He meant all that it implied. When he pulled back, he said gruffly, "I know what I'm feeling, and I think you're feeling it, too."

Haddie pulled out of his arms, and she covered her lips with her fingertips. His heart seemed to tug out of his chest toward her. He felt elated near her, and nervous, sweaty-palmed, but also like the bravest man in the world. He felt like a wreck who was capable of sweeping her into his arms and protecting her for the rest of his life. That kiss—it had been honest.

"Haddie—" His voice caught, and he swallowed. "I don't know why this happened, or what started it, but the very thought of simply walking away from you and wishing you well with your son and your business…it's almost painful. I don't want to walk away. The last time I felt anything even remotely like this was a very long time ago."

"Like what?" she breathed.

Would she force him to say it? If he had to put this tangle of conflicting emotions into words…

"Haddie… I'm not flirting or playing games. I love you."

Haddie's breath seeped out of her. She stared up at Paul, and for a moment she struggled to breathe in again. He loved her? Haddie Petersheim—the woman who was known to be a difficult match… He didn't know what he was saying.

"What?" she finally whispered.

"I know—" He looked back into her eyes helplessly. "I didn't plan it."

She put a hand on his cheek, his beard scratchy against her palm, and for a moment, she wished she could just step back into his arms, let him kiss her again and forget about all the reasons why they shouldn't do this. It had been a long, lonely two years, and she only realized now how very ready she was to be loved again. She dropped her hand.

"Haddie…" His voice was rough. "What are you thinking?"

She opened her mouth, but she couldn't put into words every last thing that swept through her mind right now.

"Do you feel it, too?" he asked at last. "Do you feel *anything* for me?"

"Why do you think I can't keep going like this?" she asked miserably. "Paul, something has started between us, but we can't let it continue!"

"So you feel it," he concluded, a smile touching his lips.

"Of course. Do you think I go around kissing men?" Her heart was filled with overwhelming emotion. "I've looked forward to seeing you every day. I like the feeling of you here in the shop with me, hearing you sawing or banging on something…" She smiled wistfully. "I've grown…too fond of you being here."

Paul tugged her closer again, and his lips hovered over hers. It would be so easy to do this—

"No." She pulled back, and he released her, his warm fingers falling away from hers.

"I know this might be painful for me to hear, but…" He seemed to brace himself. "Do you love me, Haddie? Or not?"

"*Yah*, I do love you…" Haddie's hand closed over his fingers. "It doesn't matter, though. We're too different, you and me. You know that, don't you? Everyone else could see it back when we were young."

"Your *daet* was a very good man, but he was wrong about me, Haddie," he said.

"No, he wasn't…"

"I think I'd know," he replied with a small smile.

"Leah wasn't a bad woman!" Haddie insisted, her voice firm.

"I never said she was—"

"And I had a little too much in common with her," Haddie went on. "I had a chance to talk to your daughter on Sunday, and she was talking about her late *mamm*. She was a strong-minded woman who made mistakes— I'll not pretend she didn't—but at the end of the day, she was very much like me. Had I been in her position, shunned with a baby on the way, I might have done the same things."

"Hidden our daughter?" he asked, the hurt shining in his eyes.

"I don't know…" She shook her head. "I understand her fear of losing her child. And I understand her resolve to do anything she could to raise her little girl. And I understand that strong personality that just won't knuckle under. I do…"

"This isn't about Leah…" His voice shook.

"No, it's about *me*," Haddie said. "You, Paul, are a dear, sweet man. You deserve a good, happy marriage at long last."

"I deserve a choice in who I love," he said.

Haddie met his gaze, searching for some hidden meaning behind the words, some joke perhaps, but he met her gaze evenly.

"And you'd choose me?" she whispered.

"I didn't mean to fall for you, Haddie," he said.

"I'm more difficult than other women, Paul," she said. "That's just the truth of it. I have opinions, and I won't even pretend that I'd hide them. Not at this point. I'm old enough to know that I am who I am. I know my strengths, and my weaknesses."

Paul sighed. "You don't scare me, Haddie."

"Maybe I should," she said, swallowing hard. "We've both been married before. We know how hard it is. Marriage takes work, compromise and dedication. It takes learning to understand another person inside and out, and accepting them as they are. It's not easy. Marriage is holy because it is possibly the hardest thing *Gott* asks of us."

"Maybe it isn't supposed to be that hard," Paul replied with a frown.

"If it isn't—" a lump rose in her throat "—then you should find a woman where it *would* be easier. You've been loyal to a difficult wife, Paul. You did the right thing—you deserve better now."

Paul ran a finger down her cheek, and tears misted his eyes. "Falling for me—that doesn't sway you at all?"

How she longed to say that it did! Because if she could just follow her heart, it would lead her right into Paul's arms. But she knew well enough that love was more than a courtship, more than a wedding filled with happy guests and solemn promises. Love then turned into the ins and outs of an everyday marriage, and that was where things got more difficult.

"Oh, it sways me like a reed in the wind," she breathed. "But I know my strengths. I can make an indulgent older man happy, and I never want to be the woman that a man regrets marrying. Denying myself a life with you—this breaks my heart. But becoming the woman who is your cross to bear? That would crush me, Paul!"

There was a knock on the front door, and she looked out to see a couple of people shading their eyes to look in the window. Her customers had come back, and for that she should be grateful.

"Haddie—" Paul began.

She shook her head and took another purposeful step back. "People can see us. We have reputations to consider."

Because they weren't young and foolish anymore—they were grown. They understood life and consequences better than any of the young couples making the same decisions. And Haddie knew that ultimately, they would both go on to marry others, regardless of this spontaneous love that had blossomed between them so inconveniently.

Reputations definitely mattered in this moment.

"Can we talk about this more?" he asked, his voice pleading.

"Is there anything else to say?" Haddie wiped a tear from her cheek.

Paul turned and picked up his tool bag. He stroked Barnabas's head affectionately, then headed for the front door. He flicked open the lock and turned the sign for her, then slipped outside as the customers came in.

"You're back!" Ellen Troyer said, but she leaned to the side to watch Paul disappear down the sidewalk through the big front window. An *Englisher* woman got to the counter first, and Haddie sold her the butter she required, as well as a little butter dish and some serving knives.

Haddie tried to smile through it all, and she thought she managed it serving the next several people in line, but when Ellen Troyer came up at the end of the line, Haddie felt her chin quiver.

"Haddie…" Ellen said softly. "What's happened?"

"Nothing." Haddie swallowed hard. "You need butter, don't you?"

Ellen put a hand over Haddie's. "You look ready to sob!"

Haddie wiped a stray tear from her cheek, not trusting herself with words.

"Come here—" Ellen came around the counter and held out her arms. "Come on."

Haddie didn't have it in her to fight the offered comfort, and she allowed Ellen to wrap her arms around her and the smaller woman rocked her back and forth.

"You'll be okay, Haddie," Ellen murmured. "No one is stronger than you. I know that for a fact. You'll be okay…"

Had Ellen guessed what had happened? Haddie wondered. Because Haddie didn't think she'd hidden things very well, and that made this worse. Timothy would miss Paul, and so would she. And she couldn't even hide behind appearances and keep her sadness to herself.

Haddie pulled back as the bell above the door jangled and another customer came into shop.

"I know what you need," Ellen said.

"Oh?" Haddie wished she felt that certain about her own needs right now, because her heart was still following after Paul. She let her gaze flow over his handiwork in the shop. She'd never be able to forget him now... There would be no brushing him aside, would there?

"You need an evening without cooking," Ellen said firmly. "And Timothy would love pizza, no doubt."

Haddie smiled faintly. "It's not in the budget, I'm afraid."

"That's what friends are for, Haddie," Ellen said. "I'll order it myself. It'll be delivered to the store at closing. And if you need to talk, I hope you'll come find me. I've got a sympathetic ear and an unending pot of tea."

"Thank you, Ellen," Haddie said, wiping her eyes. "You're a good friend."

Ellen headed for the door, and Haddie wiped her cheeks once more, then pasted a smile to her face as she greeted her next customers— an older *Englisher* couple.

"What can I get you today?"

"Are you okay?" the older woman asked gently.

"*Yah*. Thank you," Haddie said. "I'm fine. Just an emotional moment."

Because come what may, Haddie needed paying customers, too. Her heart might be broken, but she had bills to pay and a growing son to feed. She understood grief. It would get easier over time.

As she pulled out the scale to weigh her customer's order, her gaze fell on the engraved plate.

Honesty was blessed by *Gott*, and honesty wasn't only about scales and weights. It was also about what a woman could give. Haddie had been honest with Paul, both in her love for him and in her rejection.

Hopefully one day he'd appreciate what she'd given up to do the right thing. Integrity, while noble, was agony.

Chapter Thirteen

Paul's heart was heavy that afternoon as he drove his buggy toward Cecily's home. He was on his way to see his daughter and granddaughter, because no matter how torn up he was inside, he had a family that needed him.

Paul had known that telling Haddie how he felt was no guarantee that she'd feel the same way. Whatever had been growing between them certainly wasn't planned…and perhaps he should have seen that it wouldn't work. Call him naive or just plain stupid, but he'd seen something in Haddie this last week that he'd never seen in her before—the gentleness, the heartbreak. Was she right, and he was just repeating old mistakes, falling for a woman who'd never be a good match for him?

It had been a relief to discover that he wasn't the cruel beast Leah had believed he was. And yet, Haddie wasn't willing to take a chance on him, either. He wasn't sure where this left him, except for heartbroken. Because what he felt for Haddie right now was real. This was no boyish infatuation. And Haddie deserved to be loved deeply and completely. Forgive him, but he didn't think any other man would be able to manage it quite the way he could.

But convince Haddie of that...

He roused himself out of his thoughts. *Could* he convince her of it?

Cecily's house was coming up, and as he turned into the drive, he spotted a car parked next to the house. Abigail stood with the same group of teens from earlier. She wore that same puffy pink coat, and her hair hung down around her shoulders. She was wearing obvious makeup—something that looked out of place here at an Amish home. Abigail's friends were standing there, hands in their pockets, glaring at the house as if the very walls had wronged them. Cecily was nowhere to be seen, nor was the baby. Something was wrong here—he could feel it in his stomach.

Paul reined in his horse next to the car, close enough that he could hear the teenagers talking. They eyed him in annoyance, but didn't acknowledge him.

"This is barbaric," one said. "You can't even

charge your cell phone! What do they expect you to do all day?"

"I don't know why you even put up with this," one girl said. "You don't belong here."

Paul jumped down from his buggy, and Abigail looked up, meeting his gaze. She looked worried, uncertain.

"Abigail?" Paul said.

She didn't answer him, and her friends moved closer to her.

"They're locking you up here," one friend said, lowering his voice. "This is insane."

"Abigail is not locked up here," Paul said, raising his voice. "She's come here by her own free will."

"Can you leave?" the girl asked Abigail, her tone sarcastic.

"Well, the social-services people—"

"See? You can't go! They've locked you down!"

Paul's irritation started to rise. "She's here taking care of her daughter."

"Then leave the baby," one of the young men said, casting a glare in Paul's direction. "You don't need to do this! I'm sure they'll take care of it."

"Her," Abigail said softly. "My daughter is not an it."

"Whatever. You know what I mean. You

know you don't belong here. This is back-ward!"

Abigail looked furtively toward the house again, but she didn't answer right away. Paul stayed silent, waiting for her to speak, but Abigail didn't say anything.

"You're bad at this," the girl said. "Come on, you know it! And who expects you to be some full-time, stay-at-home mother at seventeen? This is abuse!"

They were trying to talk her into abandoning her child again, and suddenly Paul could see the pressures that had driven his daughter to leaving Taylor on that Amish doorstep. She didn't want to, but she was listening to the wrong people! They didn't know her, and they didn't care about her heart! They cared about parties and "fun."

"Abigail is not bad at this!" Paul snapped. "She's a loving, attentive mother! Babies are hard work, and sometimes mothers need a little bit of time to themselves, but that doesn't make Abigail a bad *mamm*. She adores her daughter, and she does belong here! We're her family!"

"Since when are you family?" the girl retorted, raising her voice. "You haven't been in her life! She's been on her own! She's got us!"

"And what use are you?" Paul's hands were

shaking. "You tell her she's a bad mother—that's a lie! You tell her she doesn't belong here—another lie! She belongs here more than anywhere else on this earth, because this is where her family is! We love Abigail, and while I didn't know about her until recently, that changes nothing. She's my daughter, and she will have a home here in Redemption for as long as she lives!"

Paul only realized then how loud his voice had grown, because it reverberated off the side of the house.

"Abigail…" He softened his tone. "What do you want? Forget what your friends want you to do. What do *you* want?"

Tears welled in Abigail's eyes, and just then, Taylor's crying started up from inside the house. It was a plaintive cry, filtering out from the upstairs, and Paul saw Abigail physically lean toward the house, toward her baby.

"I want to be a good mom," she whispered.

That was all Paul needed. He turned to her friends, his anger only barely capped.

"I want you to get off this property," Paul growled.

"Or what?" one of the boys said belligerently, and Paul took a step toward him. The boy immediately fell back.

"Get off this property, and leave my daughter alone!" Paul barked. "Unless my daughter calls you, you stay away! Do you hear me? Or you will deal with me!"

Paul was standing between the teens and their car, and they tried to stay as far from him as possible as they circled around him and got back into the vehicle. Once inside, their bravery returned, and they unrolled the windows.

"Abigail, just come with us!" the boy shouted. "Get in!"

Paul took another step toward the car, and the boy put it in Reverse and backed out, the tires spinning gravel up into the air. The horse took a step sideways at the spray of grit. As the car disappeared onto the road, Paul looked back toward his daughter.

Taylor's crying suddenly grew louder as the side door opened and Cecily came outside, the infant in her arms. Abigail rushed toward her and gathered her daughter into her arms, burying her face into the blankets.

"What's happening out here?" Cecily asked. "I thought you were just talking to your friends."

"They were trying to convince her to abandon her baby again," Paul said, and he met Cecily's shocked gaze. "I told them to leave."

"Come inside," Cecily said. "Oh, my! This is too much! Just come in and—"

"Can I talk to my daughter for a few minutes?" Paul asked. "Alone?"

Cecily paused, obviously upset by the whole thing, but she nodded, and went back into the house. When the screen door shut, Paul put an arm around Abigail's shoulders.

"You are a good mother," he said quietly.

"I'm not," she whispered.

"Out there in the world, they say you have to do it all on your own, and if you can't do it well by yourself, then you've failed," he said.

Abigail's chin trembled.

"That's a lie," he went on. "Families need each other. All of us! None of us can do it on our own. There's no way. No one expects you to be able to take care of your daughter, take care of yourself, keep a home, work a job… That's too much, Abigail. We're here to help you, not because you've failed, but because this is how it is. You are a good mother—and you need us, too."

Abigail sucked in a shuddering breath. "I didn't want to leave her again."

"I know," he said. "That's why I told them to leave. Anyone who tears you down shouldn't be in your life. You need people who think you're wonderful…and for the record?"

She looked up at him.

"I think you're wonderful," he said, tears misting his sight.

Abigail pressed a kiss onto her daughter's head, and the baby settled quietly into her mother's arms.

"Did I overstep in bellowing at them?" he asked. "I seem to do that a lot lately..."

"No," Abigail said. "I don't remember the last time someone cared enough to fight for me."

"Really?" He frowned.

"Well, since Mom died, at least."

Paul nodded. "You belong here, Abigail. You don't have to be Amish to be my daughter. You can go to high school, and college, and you can find your own path, and you will still be my daughter."

"Do you mean that?" she whispered.

"*Yah*. I do."

Abigail tipped her head onto Paul's shoulder. "What's that you guys call a father— *Daet*?"

"That's right." He smiled. "I'm your *daet*."

"Okay..." She smiled. *"Daet."*

He liked the sound of that, but her words were reverberating through his head. She said that it had been a long time since someone had been willing to fight for her. And that seemed to be what she needed—someone to care enough to throw his whole heart into defending her.

Maybe, just maybe, Haddie could appreciate the same thing. She seemed to be scared that she'd be too strong for him—well, maybe she needed to see him put some strength into his own feelings. He didn't need a meek wife, he needed an honest one! He needed a woman who would tell him straight when her feelings were hurt, or when he went wrong. He needed a woman willing to fight for their marriage just as strongly as he would.

It wasn't about meekness, it was about loyalty!

"Let's get you inside, where it's warm," Paul said. "Because I have something I need to discuss with you and *Mammi*."

"Oh?" Abigail looked up at him.

"I have a woman I'd like to marry," he said, "but you're my daughter, and you'll be a part of this new family if she'll consent to be mine...to be *ours*."

"The butter maker?" Abigail asked.

Paul looked at her in surprise.

"You don't hide things well," Abigail said with a smile. "And I like her. She was really kind to me."

He'd have to see if he could show Haddie exactly what she meant to him, because

Haddie Petersheim's strength wasn't going to scare him off. If she'd be willing to use that strength for their shared family, he'd count himself blessed.

The next morning was cold, and snowflakes drifted down from the sky as Haddie steered their horse into the drive that led to the schoolhouse. She hadn't slept well the night before. Despite her earnest prayer that *Gott* would take whatever she was feeling for Paul away, *Gott* hadn't answered. Instead, all she could think about were his gentle eyes, his strong hands and the way he made her stomach flutter when he kissed her.

Was it a test of her strength?

This morning, she and Timothy were dropping off the finished bench. Betty Beiler was there early, as always, and Haddie could see the four Lapp boys trudging down the road from the other direction, on their way to school.

"You did a good job on this bench, son," Haddie said as she reined in the horses. "I'm proud of you."

Timothy smiled shyly. "*Yah*, I worked on it. Paul said I'm good at woodworking. Did you know that?"

"Did he say that?"

"*Yah*, and he says if I work hard, I could learn to make a chair, or a table, and I could look at that piece of furniture and know I made it myself. I want to try that. Do you think he could come back?"

Haddie felt the lump rise back in her throat.

"First things first," she said, trying to sound bright. "Let's show your teacher your handiwork."

Timothy helped Haddie to unload the bench, and Betty held open the schoolhouse door for them as they carried it inside.

"This is very nice work!" Betty said, leaning over the bench as they put it down. "Timothy, you should be proud of this."

They took a few minutes to look over the bench together, and Betty admired the craftsmanship, pointing out the tight seams and how it didn't wobble even a little. Timothy's chest rose a little higher at his teacher's obvious pleasure over the new bench.

"I'm very sorry I broke the last one," Timothy said, clasping his hands in front of him. "It was wrong of me to be fooling around like that, and I won't be doing that again. I'm going to work hard, and if you'll give me another chance—"

"Timothy." The teacher bent down to look him in the face. "Every time you say you're sorry you get another chance with me. That's how *Gott* works, and that's how I work. I'm proud of you. Today is a fresh day."

Haddie's eyes misted as she saw her son's shoulders straighten. Forgiveness was a powerful thing indeed.

"Go on out and play," Betty said with a smile. "You boys are building a snow fort, aren't you?"

Timothy grinned and dashed for the door. "Thank you!"

Out the window, she saw the Lapp boys toss aside their schoolbags and run to join Timothy.

"Timothy has been talking about Paul Ebersole helping him build that bench for days," Betty said. "It really seems to mean a lot to him. And Paul is a good man."

"*Yah*, he is," Haddie agreed. "Did you see his daughter on service Sunday?"

"*Yah*. I didn't get to talk with her," Betty replied. "But I've heard she's a sweet girl. She's lost a lot. I remember when you and Paul were stepping out together. When Leah left, I told my husband over and over again that if Paul had married you it would have been different."

"I'm actually a little too much like Leah," Haddie said with an uncomfortable laugh.

"How?" Betty frowned.

"We were both very strong personalities,"

Haddie said. "We had strong opinions. Paul needed a milder girl than either of us were."

"Hmm." Betty shook her head slowly. "There I disagree. Paul isn't a mild man, himself. That was his problem with Leah. They were both strong in their own ways, but it takes true strength to *stay*. Leah didn't want an Amish life deep down. It chafed at her. I used to babysit her with my own daughters, you know. And Leah always was a little drawn to anything *English*. She enjoyed being contrary. She thought it made her special."

"Oh… I didn't realize that. I didn't know her terribly well."

"Paul, on the other hand, was stubborn, too," Betty said. "And I'd like to see him married again, but he'll need a woman strong enough to match him. Strength looks different in different people, you see. Some are more outspoken, and others just dig in their heels. He's the second type."

"That's not very promising, is it?" Haddie asked.

"Well, it depends on what he digs in his heels for," Betty replied. "If he's determinedly *yours*…"

A smile touched Betty's lips, and Haddie felt her face heat. How much did the schoolteacher know? Had rumors spread? Had people seen them through the window when he'd kissed her? Possibilities swirled through her head.

"Now, I'm only guessing, but from the stories Timothy told at school, Paul is sweet on you, Haddie."

"I'm a strong woman," Haddie said. "My father warned me that certain men couldn't handle it."

"Certain men can't," Betty said with a nod. "But the best ones can."

She shot Haddie a smile, and the school door opened, two little girls coming inside, chattering together.

"I have to go open the shop," Haddie said. "I'll be late for the cream."

She'd be late for Paul...and her heart gave a little leap at the thought. Was it possible that their stubbornness could be their strength? Was she running from a man strong enough to match her, too?

She was afraid of making him miserable over time, but what if they could be the perfect balance for each other, strength balancing strength?

She hoisted herself up into her buggy and waved at Timothy, who was busy packing snow into a wall, and he waved back. Then she guided the horse around and they headed up toward the road.

Gott, *I don't know why I can't stop loving him*, she prayed in her heart. *Is this possibly Your will?*

And in the whisper of winter wind, she felt a flood of peace. Her love for Paul had not diminished, but her fear had.

Chapter Fourteen

Haddie wasn't at her shop when he arrived there that morning, and he left the cream next to her side door, where she'd find it. He waited around for a few minutes, and then headed back the way he'd come.

Maybe it was for the best, Paul realized. If he was going to say his piece, he wanted to be dressed for it, anyway. If he was going to ask a woman to vow to be his, he should be in his newest shirt and pants, at the very least.

So he returned later that morning with a bunch of flowers that he picked up from a local shop. There were no other customers there when he came inside, the bell tinkling cheerfully overhead. He spotted Haddie stocking a shelf with cookbooks. Her eyes looked red-rimmed, and his heart sped up.

"Haddie? Are you okay?"

Haddie rose to her feet, her gaze dropping to the flowers at his side. He held them out to her, and she took them with a smile.

"I missed you," she said. "I got used to you being here… Isn't that silly?"

Paul bent down and kissed her lips tenderly, and she looked up at him questioningly.

"Haddie, I'm going to ask you something, and I need you to let me say my whole piece," he said.

"Okay…"

"Now, I know you think you're too strong for me, but here's the thing…" He sucked in a deep breath. "You're not."

She blinked at him. "Oh…"

"I mean, you *are* strong, Haddie—" He winced, then looked down at the flowers in her hands. This had come out better when he'd rehearsed it on the ride over. "But I love that about you. That's what I'm trying to say. I don't need a woman to meekly agree with me. I need a woman who can help me think things through. And I know you can handle yourself, your son, your business… It's no question of what you're capable of. But I want to make things easier for you. I want to be the man who lightens your burdens and make it so that you don't have to be so strong all the time. I want to be the man who you can lean on, Haddie."

Haddie lifted the flowers to her face, then raised her gaze to meet his. "Are you sure about that?"

"*Yah*, I'm sure."

The bell above the door tinkled, and Paul turned to see an *Englisher* man come into the shop.

"We'll just be a minute," Paul said in English, and he turned back to Haddie, speaking in Pennsylvania Dutch. "I have to say this, Haddie. I love you. I want to marry you, and I know you're a strong woman, but I trust in your character. I know I fought with Leah, but I'm more mature now, and I will promise you that I'll never fight you. I'll only fight for us—you, me and our children. If you could be a mother to my daughter, too."

Was that all of it? He searched himself for more words, but came up empty. Behind them the bell jangled again, and he heard more people enter the shop. He closed his eyes and grimaced. He really didn't need an audience for this!

"I love you, too, Paul," Haddie said. "And, *yah*, I'd be honored to be Abigail's stepmother. I love her already!"

Paul blinked. That sounded like a yes… It sounded very close to a yes. He wanted to kiss her then, but he needed a direct answer before it was official.

"So…" Paul swallowed. "What do you say? Will you marry me? Will you be my wife?"

"Yah!"

That was what he needed to hear, and he gathered her up in his arms, and lowered his lips over hers. He heard murmurs of surprise behind him, but he didn't care.

"They just got engaged!" a familiar woman's voice said, and he broke off the kiss and turned to see Cecily standing there, her hands clasped in front of her and a smile on her face.

"Congratulations!" That was from an *Englisher* man, and there was a smattering of clapping. There were more customers gathered there than he'd realized.

"Normally, we keep engagements a secret," Paul said in English. "I'm not sure I managed that." He turned back to Haddie. "It's not exactly traditional, but I don't mind if people know. I'm not letting anything get in the way of our wedding."

"I don't mind at all," Haddie said, and she bustled past him toward the counter. "Now, who can I help?"

Haddie shot him a smile, her cheeks pink, and the first couple came up to the counter, overflowing with congratulations. Paul followed Haddie back behind the counter, and as they gave their order, he pulled it out of the refrigerator. He handed the rolls of butter to Haddie and she looked at him in surprise.

"It'll be a family business, after all," he said. "I'd better learn the ropes, don't you think?"

When the customers had left, Haddie leaned against the counter and looked at him in wonder.

"Are we really doing this?" she asked.

"Well, it's out there now, so I think we have to," he said, but he laughed. "Haddie, I can't wait to make you mine. I mean that. I hope… that you feel the same."

In response, Haddie slipped back into his arms and tipped her face against his chest. Her arms tightened around his waist.

"Me, too," she whispered.

He wrapped his arms around her, and with his arms came his heart, too. The first Tuesday that the bishop could manage it, he wanted to marry this woman. He'd waited long enough for the real kind of love he'd been aching for, and now that he'd found it, he felt strangely at peace.

Paul looked down at Haddie, and she tipped her face up to smile at him.

In Haddie's arms, he'd just found home.

Epilogue

The wedding was held on the Ebersole farm
that spring when the grass was lush and green,
and the trees had sprouted their first tender
leaves. The engagement had not been a secret
at all, and the entire community of Redemption joined in the fun of planning for their big
day. Haddie had involved Abigail as much as
she could, too, and they'd spent many an afternoon working on a wedding quilt together—
the few patches that Abigail had stitched being
a little crooked, and the stitches uneven.

"It doesn't have to be straight to be perfect,"
Haddie told Paul when she showed him their
progress. "This will be our family, and these
are Abigail's first quilt blocks. I'm proud of
her. I'm glad they're in our wedding quilt."

Her open heart toward his daughter and
granddaughter only made him love her more.

Ellen Troyer helped Haddie make her dress, and Miriam Lapp came by to pitch in with a thorough cleaning of the house, since Paul and Haddie would be living in her house. There was more privacy for them as a little family there, and Paul preferred it that way. He wanted as much time alone with his new wife as he could get.

By the wedding day, everything was ready, and everyone in Redemption was equally excited to see Paul and Haddie finally take their vows.

Haddie was in the farmhouse doing whatever women did to get ready for these things, and Paul, standing at the barn door, looked back across the yard to where the church benches had all been set up, and families were milling around talking with each other, waiting for the service to start.

Inside the barn, Timothy was wearing his best church clothes, which already had a dusty smear up one pant leg. He squatted next to a pen that held a bottle-fed calf, his shoulders stooped.

"You okay in there?" Paul asked.

Timothy startled and turned around. *"Yah."*

"You look… I don't know…sad," Paul said.

"It's going to be different now," Timothy replied. "It was me and *Mamm*, and now you'll be there, and it won't be the same. I was the man of the house."

"Ah." Paul came into the barn and leaned against the side of the pen. He reached down and scratched the top of the calf's head. "There are a few jobs that are too big for you, though, and that's where I come in."

"Like what?"

"Like making money to support you, and making it so that your *mamm* doesn't have to work so hard," he replied.

"I'm in school. I can't help it."

"I know. And you should be in school. You need to be a kid—having fun, learning things. And it's my job now to make sure you can do that."

"Hmm." Timothy sighed.

"Here's the thing, Timothy," Paul said quietly. "We both love your *mamm* a lot, and we both want to see her happy, right?"

"Yah," Timothy agreed.

"So let's work together on that. I'm going to do all the things grown up men can do, like working hard and being kind to her and making her smile, and you can do the same. You'll work hard at school, and not sass back, and between the two of us, we'll make sure your *mamm* is the happiest woman in Redemption."

"Okay." Timothy stood up. "*Yah*, okay… That will work."

Paul smiled. "I'm not only here for your *mamm*, though. I'm here to help you, too. I'll teach you more woodworking, and we'll get you milking before long, too. And—" Paul swallowed "—if you have any problems at all with bullies or anything like that, I'm here to be the *daet* at your back."

Timothy shrugged. "They're already pretty scared of my *mamm*."

Paul couldn't help but chuckle. "You could let me try, at least."

"We'll see." But Timothy grinned then, and Paul tapped the top of the boy's hat.

"We'll have a happy family, Timothy," Paul said, and he looked in the direction of the barn door and the bright spring sunshine beyond it. "But your *mamm* will be a whole lot less happy if they can't find us for the ceremony."

"Uh-oh!" Timothy headed for the barn door. "Are we late?"

"We will be if we don't get moving," Paul replied.

Timothy headed outside, and Paul followed, pulling the barn door shut behind him. There was still a streak of dirt up one side of Timothy's pant leg, and Ellen Troyer seemed to spot it all the way across the yard, because within a minute she had a cloth and was crouched next to Timothy, wiping it off again.

"It's a wedding, Timothy!" Ellen chided. "Can't you stay clean?"

Timothy stood patiently as Ellen cleaned his leg, and cast Paul a sheepish smile.

It was a wedding, indeed, and Paul sucked in a wavering breath. He was about to vow to be Haddie's for as long as he should live, but as Haddie stepped outside the house in her new, blue wedding dress, her hands clasped in front of her, and her cheeks pink, all those jittering nerves suddenly stilled. She was just so beautiful…

Help me to love her well, he prayed in his heart.

It seemed like the best thing he could ask of *Gott*. Because this next blessed stage of his life began and ended with the heart of this one woman. She would be the center of his family, and her smile would be his reward at the end of a long day of work. She'd be the one to hold his fragile heart as he took this first step into a different kind of marriage, and Paul felt a surge of gratefulness so deep that it brought tears to his eyes.

He couldn't wait to make her his.

* * * * *

Dear Reader,

I hope you enjoy this latest story from the town of Redemption, Pennsylvania. I certainly enjoy writing them!

If you'd like to find me online, I do a constant stream of giveaways with other sweet romance authors on my Facebook page. You can also find me on Bookbub and Twitter. I love hearing from my readers, so come by and join the fun! You can also find me on my website, patriciajohns.com, where you can find all of my backlist books. You never know—you might find your next read!

Patricia

Get 4 FREE REWARDS!

We'll send you 2 FREE Books plus 2 FREE Mystery Gifts.

Love Inspired books feature uplifting stories where faith helps guide you through life's challenges and discover the promise of a new beginning.

FREE
Value Over
$20

Get 4 FREE REWARDS!

We'll send you 2 FREE Books plus 2 FREE Mystery Gifts.

Harlequin Heartwarming Larger-Print books will connect you to uplifting stories where the bonds of friendship, family and community unite.

FREE
Value Over
$20

COMING NEXT MONTH FROM
Love Inspired

THEIR SECRET COURTSHIP
by Emma Miller

Resisting pressure from her mother to marry, Bay Stutzman is determined to keep her life exactly as it is. Until Mennonite David Jansen accidentally runs her wagon off the road. Now Bay must decide whether sharing a life with David is worth leaving behind everything she's ever known...

CARING FOR HER AMISH FAMILY
The Amish of New Hope • by Carrie Lighte

Forced to move into a dilapidated old house when entrusted with caring for her *Englisch* nephew, Amish apron maker Anke Bachman must turn to newcomer Josiah Mast for help with repairs. Afraid of being judged by his new community, Josiah tries to distance himself from the pair but can't stop his feelings from blossoming...

FINDING HER WAY BACK
K-9 Companions • by Lisa Carter

After a tragic event leaves widower Detective Rob Melbourne injured and his little girl emotionally scarred, he enlists the services of therapy dog handler Juliet Newkirk and her dog, Moose. But will working with the woman he once loved prove to be a distraction for Rob...or the second chance his family needs?

THE REBEL'S RETURN
The Ranchers of Gabriel Bend • by Myra Johnson

When a family injury calls him home to Gabriel Bend, Samuel Navarro shocks everyone by arriving with a baby in tow. His childhood love, Joella James, reluctantly agrees to babysit his infant daughter. But can they forget their tangled past and discover a future with this newly devoted father?

AN ORPHAN'S HOPE
by Christina Miller

Twice left at the altar, preacher Jase Armstrong avoids commitment at all costs—until he inherits his cousin's three-day-old baby. Pushing him further out of his comfort zone is nurse Erin Tucker and her lessons on caring for an infant. But can Erin convince him he's worthy of being a father *and* a husband?

HER SMALL-TOWN REFUGE
by Jennifer Slattery

Seeking a fresh start, Stephanie Thornton and her daughter head to Sage Creek. But when the veterinary clinic where she works is robbed, all evidence points to Stephanie. Proving her innocence to her boss, Caden Stoughton, might lead to the new life she's been searching for...

LICNM0122A